APOCALYPSE

Other Books in This Series from Peter and Paul Lalonde

Revelation (Book #2)

Tribulation (Book #3)

Judgment (Book #4)

APOCALYPSE

PETER AND PAUL LALONDE

THOMAS NELSON PUBLISHERS®
Nashville

Published in Nashville, Tennessee, by Thomas Nelson, Inc.

Scripture quotations are from the following sources:

The KING JAMES VERSION of the Bible.

Library of Congress-in-Publication Data

Lalonde, Peter.
    Apocalypse / Peter and Paul Lalonde.
        p. cm.
    ISBN 0-7852-6686-0
    1. Rapture (Christian eschatology)—Fiction. 2. Television news
anchors—Fiction. 3. End of the world—Fiction. I. Lalonde, Paul,
1961– II. Title.
    PS.3562.A4147 A87 2001
    813'.54—dc21   2001030799
                                                              CIP

Printed in the United States of America.

01 02 03 04 PHX 5 4 3 2 1

Prologue

IN THE TROUBLED TIMES THAT WOULD FOLLOW when the very foundations of earth seemed to shake and crumble, Abdallah would insist that what had happened to his son was God's will. He would recite the sacred words of ritual praise remembered since his childhood, holding back the tears for later when he could share his grief with his wife.

The days turned to weeks, and his prayers continued, but as the turmoil and strife of these events that tore apart his homeland continued to unfold, Abdallah in his heart would truly come to believe the words he had spoken.

He and his son had left that morning, invoking God's name for their journey, as was the custom among his people. "Promise you and Ahmed will not be late returning home tonight," his wife, Perichehr, pleaded.

"No. The boy has much work to do and the journey is tiring," replied Abdallah. "We will return before sunset, *Insha'allah.*" The words meant "God willing," and though he spoke them frequently, they were always said with conviction. For Bedouins like Abdallah, as for so many other

Arabs, God was supreme. They did not plan their futures. Fate could neither be known nor altered. They concerned themselves with the moment, and that moment had been an auspicious one.

The trek to Megiddo through the Jezreel Valley of Israel, the sacred and historic site of so many past civilizations, was, and always had been, a joyous celebration of God's people in all their diversity. He pointed out to his son the Lebanese, Ja'bari, Kurds, Samaritans, Vietnamese, Masri, Syrians, Ethiopian Copts, American Mormons, Maronites, evangelical Christian fundamentalists, and many others they met along the way as they passed a flourishing Jewish kibbutz. All were drawn to this site with its more than six thousand years of history, layered in sequences the archaeologists had only recently begun to uncover.

"Do you see that mound of rocks, Ahmed?" asked Abdallah, pointing to the remains of one of several buildings. "This temple is over five thousand years old."

"Was that where Grandfather prayed to Allah when he was a boy?" asked the child with a note of awe.

"That temple is older than your grandfather." Abdallah laughed. "It is older than his grandfather. Even older than the time of the prophet Muhammad." He wanted to tell the boy of the full history of this land, the history of the Creator's hand in the lives of all men who called on Him uttering the name Allah or Yahweh, the Lord Almighty, or any of a dozen other names. Here were the ruins of temples and cities, each built upon the other, each bearing the witness of peace and war, love and hate, hope and frustration, fear and rejoicing.

The location of Megiddo made it a natural passageway for armies bent on conquest, and Abdallah recited the tales of the great warriors of the past. He told his son of Thutmose III, who came to Megiddo to conquer a civilization so rich that it was written that he carried away 2,000 head of cattle, 400 horses, 900 carriages, including 2 made of gold from the houses of the governors of Megiddo, 20,500 sheep, along with battle armor, military uniforms, archers' bows . . . The list was as endless as the years of antiquity.

"Each new city was built upon the old," Abdallah explained. "The day will come when you will read of men such as Thutmose and King David, Ahab and King Solomon, King Josiah and Pharaoh Necho. You will see the hand of Allah bestowing peace on stubborn people who only kept returning to war. You will see how each layer of these ruins, each city built upon a city past, represents new hope for the people of this land."

The boy did not understand. He was too young. Ahmed wanted only to toss pebbles over the edge of the archaeological digs to see how far they would drop. But his father still had to begin the process of teaching his son a way different from that of his own father, whose passionate anger turned to hatred as he saw his beloved Palestine become an occupied territory. As an old man, he would curse the day he first heard the Jewish term "Eretz Israel," the land promised by God. He cursed as well the Christians who saw this

land as that of Jesus' ministry but failed to even acknowl-
edge Muhammad.

Abdallah thought differently. The ruins of Megiddo,
the shades and colors of its visitors, all reminded him of
God's vast creation. Rather than being angered by the difference of names of God, he rejoiced that so many people
were coming to worship the one true Creator. He had read
not just the Koran, but the Bible as well. He had seen that
Mary, the mother of Jesus, was mentioned more times in
his people's holy book than in the New Testament. He realized that there was a deeper message for those who would
only try to see and understand.

While others were drawn to the Temple Mount in
Jerusalem where three faiths had fought for so long over the
name of God, he came here to Megiddo. The excavation
always made him feel as though he was in touch with the
lives and destinies of the world, preparing him for something new and preordained.

"You are a foolish man," his wife had teasingly told him.
She knew it was wrong to speak against the teachings of the
elders. But she also knew that her husband was a man of
deep devotion. What did it matter if he took his only son
from the sheep and the cattle for a few hours? They would
return before sunset, *Insha'allah*, happy for the day they had
together.

◦◦◦

The woman from the tourist bus saw him first. Although he
was not in uniform, the tour guide had explained how all

Israelis are trained for the army at eighteen. They could be called to active duty at any time, and they frequently went out on patrol in civilian dress. It was why so many men and women carried weapons, rifles having replaced the swords of other eras awaiting the return of the Messiah when He would beat them into plowshares.

The woman wanted to take a photo of the soldier and asked her husband if he thought it would be rude to ask. She had already snapped a picture of the Bedouin father and son, something the tour guide admonished her against. Such casual photographing without permission violated Arab sensibilities, and she did not want to offend anyone else.

"Everybody takes pictures of the soldiers," her husband replied. "I saw it done in Jerusalem and Tel Aviv and in Nazareth. Why should this place be any different?"

The woman shrugged, picking up her camera and turned toward the man now cradling his weapon in his arms. She waved to him, hoping to get him to look her way. But when he started to turn, it was too late to realize that he was not posing but starting to aim his rifle straight at her.

For an instant all was frozen. The tour guide held a microphone, telling the tourists that their bus would depart in five minutes. The Arab man was laughing at his son, who had thrown a pebble at a bird that now dived down on him, angrily squawking its displeasure. The woman continued to shoot frame after frame as, nearby an Israeli couple leaned against a tree, drinking something cold before starting back to their kibbutz.

In the next moment, horror and shock erupted. A bullet

shattered the knee of the woman with the camera, sending her plunging to the ground, screaming in agony. A window of the tour bus exploded, shards of glass peppering the driver's face like slashing razors. Several Israelis rushed at the gunman, grabbing his weapon, raining down blows until he dropped to the ground. Using a belt they bound his wrists. As Abdallah watched in terror, he turned to see Ahmed, his only son, sprawled on the ground, the earth beneath turning red from the blood pouring from a gaping head wound.

"Ahmed!" he screamed, running desperately to the fallen child. "Ahmed!"

Abdallah realized there was no hope even before he reached the lifeless figure, even before someone from the tour bus, identifying herself as a retired nurse, pronounced his child beyond help. He could not tell if the shooter was an Arab or a Jew. He did not know if he was a terrorist or a man driven insane with the anger that infected this land nor did he care. Cradling his son's head and crying out to the living God, he could only ask, "Why?" over and over again.

His faith told him that death was not the end, a belief echoed by the other holy books he had secretly read in his youth. Ahmed would be in a joyous place in the arms of a Father who had lost His own Son for the sins of this world. Abdallah understood all this, but it didn't matter. His grief crushed him like a stone

Within minutes people were swarming about the site, some with guns, some with medical kits. The residents of the kibbutz had grown accustomed to dealing with pain and violence and death. Joy and sorrow were two sides of a coin, endlessly turning in this land, buffeted by winds of change. They had learned through it all only to praise God, accepting His ultimate wisdom and justice, burying the dead, and tending to the wounded, even as they rejoiced with each new life in the endless circle of birth and death.

Abdallah heard many voices in several languages, but could understand nothing. Someone wrapped their arms about his shoulders, a stranger who did not understand his people's rituals of grief. Still Abdallah felt strangely comforted, as though his loss had touched another and this act reached beyond traditions. Why must human beings suffer tragedy before the love of God could be revealed in them?

It was then that a great light of understanding broke over him. He understood why so many Christians ignored the name of Meggido and chose to use the other name by which it was called—Armageddon.

Perhaps, after all, that explained why his only son, an innocent child in love with all creation, could meet a violent and senseless death in such a holy place. Until now, Abdallah had always rejoiced in the boundless love of the God who, time and again, allowed Megiddo to be rebuilt, each new community rising on the ruins of the previous. Now he understood that the Christians were right all along. Megiddo should be called Armageddon, a place where one day, the last battle between good and evil would be fought. He could only wonder in his deep sorrow, as so many arms reached out, so many tongues spoke strange but comforting words, if the good forces would fall short as they had this day—too late to prevent the fearful triumph of evil.

ᴔ

Even if Ginnie had asked, Lennie probably couldn't have told her why he had picked her to go to the prom. It was true that they both loved dancing, even if their skill was far exceeded by their enthusiasm.

Between them, Lennie and Ginnie had completed a collection of old Fred Astaire and Gene Kelly movies, watching enthralled as the stars danced with such partners as Ginger Rogers, Debbie Reynolds, and Cyd Charisse. Together they transform themselves into the romantic leads of *Top Hat*, *Singin' in the Rain*, *On the Town*, and so many others.

Not that their practice had helped that much. In the years they had been best friends, Ginnie had broken a big toe, had several major bruises, and a sprained ankle. Lennie had wrenched his back and received seventeen stitches that time he'd tripped over a floor lamp and put his hand through an aquarium. They both knew better than to venture onto the dance floor on prom night except, perhaps, for a slow dance or two. They might have shared a love of big band music, but classmates preferred groups whose names couldn't even be written on the prom posters. The music, of course, was even more foul.

Still, it was the prom, the last big event of high school before graduation and college. And, while Lennie knew that none of the other guys would ever consider dating a "geek" like Ginnie, with her sweaty palms, spotty face, and a pre-pubescent figure, he visibly relaxed when she said she was available. And, while Ginnie knew that the other girls made fun of Lennie's serious side, heading up an after-school Bible study club, and talking to teens about how to prepare for the end times, she, too, was relieved when he invited her.

That night they huddled in the midst of raucous sounds and colors as all around kids cavorted to sounds that reminded Ginnie of Joshua bringing down the walls of Jericho. At first they tried to talk—there was always something to say no matter how many hours they spent on the telephone.

Then they tried their best to enjoy the music, but the volume was more than the small gym could absorb. Most of the chaperones wore earplugs and those who didn't kept finding excuses to escape, if only for a few minutes.

It was then that Lennie's hand found itself holding Ginnie's for the first time since they became friends. Ginnie didn't object—it seemed so natural. His warm, reas-suring touch spoke of the sense of common destiny they both shared.

Neither was exactly aware of when they got up to leave. Lennie said something about punch. Ginnie mentioned the buffet. They moved toward the table still holding hands. And without saying a word or changing direction, they suddenly found themselves outside the gym in the cool night air.

The high school was located at the base of a hill, and

they walked slowly up a path that led to an overlook and a panorama of the Los Angeles skyline. The full moon was hazy through the smog, and shades of red and yellow still lingered from the brilliant sunset made even more spectacular by the dirty air.

With the city spread out beneath them, Lennie and Ginnie each felt alive with feelings neither could express but knew instinctively the other would understand. They reached the top of the hill and stood silently for moments that seemed like a sweet eternity. Neither was aware of time's passage, attuned instead only to each other. The emotions they knew transcended adolescent infatuation.

Their lips met, the first kiss for each, gentle and unhurried. Their hearts understood what their minds did not yet comprehend. Lennie felt her hand caress the back of his neck. Ginnie felt herself enveloped in his arms, arms that seemed so strong, so comforting, so familiar. Light-headed, pausing for breath, they kissed again as Lennie's glasses slipped from his face and the city lights became but a blur of brilliant color. A gentle quaking seemed to radiate from their toes to their heads. Ginnie smiled, then laughed with joy, kissing Lennie once more. She knew love could move mountains, but this was more like standing on a rug that had been suddenly yanked from under their feet. A sound like a freight train roared up around them.

The couple felt the ever-growing shocks. "Lennie!" Ginnie shouted, suddenly frightened and grabbing his sleeve.

"I've got you!" he replied, reaching for her arm and

bringing her near. The sensation lasted less than a minute, though it seemed much longer. When it was over, Lennie, his glasses bent and one lens popped out, looked down the hill squinting into the blurry night.

"Ginnie," he whispered. "Oh, my Lord, Ginnie." The high school that had moments before been ablaze with lights and throbbing music was now in complete darkness. By the dim glow of the moon, they could see what had once been steel, concrete, and glass had now become a pile of rubble. The destruction had been swift and total, as though the school had been constructed of children's building blocks and smashed by a sledgehammer.

As they watched, an eerie light began to flicker, growing stronger and finally bursting forth like a hellish beacon in the night sky. The remains of the school were ablaze, along with the other buildings around it. The earth was buckled and cracked by the force of the earthquake.

"I guess it was the big one," Ginnie whispered, then felt another sharp jolt. The next quake was shorter but of equal intensity, sending them tumbling down the hill together, fighting for handholds as they clutched at each other.

Coming to a stop Lennie immediately realized they would have to call for help, to try to get a rescue effort under way. In the distance they could hear the mournful wail of endless car alarms triggered by the quake. The telephone lines were probably dead, but someone was bound to have a cell phone that still worked.

It was then that they noticed the most chilling sound

of all—a deafening silence from the school gym where moments before the prom had been in full swing.

The quake had instantly created a carnage more complete than any bomb landing directly on the building.

Although Lennie and Ginnie would tear at the rubble until their hands were bleeding and their clothing in tatters; although surviving neighbors joined them with picks, shovels, and pry bars, no one, in the end, was found alive. The prom goers had all perished beneath tons of concrete and steel.

Only Ginnie and Lennie were left alive from among their classmates, and in the days that followed, their story would be repeated hundreds of times as Los Angeles struggled to feed, shelter, and comfort hundreds of thousands of people left homeless. Hope was sustained by the account of two teens who had survived a catastrophe that, in the end, would take more lives than every war Americans had fought since the Revolution.

Chapter 1

SUSAN HILDEBRANDT KNEW THEY WERE MONEY the moment they entered the Cardwell Towers leasing office. The man was tall, lean, muscular; his immaculately styled black hair was laced with gray and his Armani suit was obviously custom tailored. His supple shoes were made from unborn calf, his shirtsleeves glittered with gold and diamond cuff links and a limited-edition Rolex was worth more cash than her Cadillac. The woman, on the other hand, carried a combination overnight bag/briefcase that was neither expensive nor particularly distinctive, the type of item one could buy for less than a hundred dollars in any luggage shop.

Yet, the woman's clothes were a striking blend of the most respected couturiers in the world: a blouse from Paris, a skirt from Rome, and a long scarf, handmade by a famed London designer whose work sold for nothing less than five hundred pounds. Her shoes bore the mark of Lugano, a small shop on the Upper East Side of Manhattan where some of the most exotic leathers in the world were used to custom fit a world-class clientele.

Not that Susan could afford such items herself. Her purchases still were made at Saks and then only during sales. But it was part of her job to keep current with the places at which the tiny percentage of truly wealthy people shopped. She needed to be able to spot the differences between the merely rich and those who might want to live in Chicago's flagship apartment building owned by the notorious Spencer Cardwell.

"We realize you're almost ready to close," said the woman with a posh New England boarding school accent. "But we have to leave for Europe tomorrow and we did so want to see your suites before we left. We're spending so much time in Chicago, it seems foolish to be stranded in a hotel suite."

"No problem," replied Susan. "We're here to meet your needs. I'd be happy to show you what is available." She had been working since early that morning, catching up on her paperwork. Her feet were tired, her back ached, and she had been hoping to meet Frank at that new French restaurant everyone was talking about. But Frank would just have to understand. She was sure she had a live one.

"We only need a one-bedroom if the rest of the apartment is large enough to entertain," remarked the man. He spoke with a crisp accent that might have originated from any one of several different European countries.

"I have just the place," said Susan. "Thirty-fourth floor with a spectacular view of the lake. It's one-bedroom, but the formal dining and living rooms are almost 2,500 square feet by themselves." She did not mention price. If they had to ask, they couldn't afford it. And these people obviously did not have to ask.

"That sounds perfect," replied the woman. "We'd like to take a look at it if that's not too much trouble."

For an instant Susan thought of calling the restaurant and leaving word for Frank, but thought better of it. If these two were serious, the last thing she wanted was for them to feel rushed.

They spent an hour in the apartment and another forty-five minutes touring the building with its three restaurants, private health club, full-service dry cleaners, and even a private library of both books and videos. A full-time concierge staff, she informed them, handled any and all needs, and the security system was airtight.

"Mr. Cardwell wanted the building to be a self-contained community," she explained. "An oasis in the city for those who appreciate the very best." *And who have more money than brains*, she thought ruefully to herself. She knew several of the tenants were heirs to vast fortunes that they were doing their best to whittle down to nothing. A few were connected with various governments in exile, living on looted treasuries, and there were a few unindicted corporate CEOs under investigation. Of course, the tenants also included self-made, completely honest executives and entrepreneurs who simply enjoyed a lavish lifestyle. She had no idea to which category this couple belonged, nor did she care. They were contemplating spending more than two million dollars, and that was more than enough of a reference for Susan.

"I'd like to take another look at the suite," said the man. "If it's not too late, that is."

Susan checked her watch, 7:15 P.M. on a Sunday evening. Frank was liable to be gone by the time they finished. Even with her stomach rumbling and her body aching, she smiled and said, "I think taking another look is an excellent idea."

Susan next showed the woman a wing of the suite that could be adapted for a home office, specially wired for multiple telephone lines, cable access, and a variety of communication devices. "Many of the tenants need elaborate computer and teleconferencing systems to effectively handle their global businesses," she explained. "I think you'll find that whatever your needs, the building is equipped for . . ."

She stopped suddenly as she felt the barrel of a gun pressed to her back. There had been no change in the couple's manner, no shift in the tone of their voices. One moment they were inspecting the premises, the next they were threatening her life.

"If this is a robbery, I think you have it backward," said Susan, her voice trembling with fear. "I'm lucky if I can afford El fare. I should be robbing you."

"This is no robbery," replied the woman, moving away from Susan. She was unarmed, but from the way she instinctively balanced herself, as if ready to move swiftly in any direction, Susan suspected she was a martial arts expert. "We just need access to this building for a couple of hours, and you've been kind enough to show us how to achieve that."

"I don't understand . . . ," Susan stammered.

"You don't need to," replied the woman. When she saw that Susan was resisting, she opened her bag and put on a thin pair of leather gloves. Susan suddenly realized that the man was wearing an identical pair and recalled that neither of them had touched anything during the tour. They let Susan open doors for them, handling everything.

"We're going to need you to stay in this suite," said the man. "We don't want to be interrupted until we're finished."

Susan was silent, wary, and more than a little frightened.

"If you cooperate, you will be left unharmed," added the woman. "If you cause trouble, we will kill you. Is that clear?"

"Whatever you say," was Susan's nervous reply. Her mouth was dry and she felt as though she might faint. It was like being out of control with no way to fight back. Nothing about this couple made sense to her.

The bag about which she had been so curious contained several lengths of rope along with some canisters, tools, and electronic equipment. They tied her up securely, the ropes so taut she could not move without the cords biting into her wrists and ankles. Her shoulders ached from the strain. The woman had looped her expensive scarf twice around Susan's face, tying it between her teeth, then wrapping it again over her mouth to firmly gag her.

Susan had to fight panic in order to keep breathing. Unless she stayed calm, inhaling and exhaling carefully through her nose, she would choke from the cloth in her mouth. She dared not scream for help. All she could do was endure her fear until someone found her. There was no other alternative.

Moving swiftly through the building to the maintenance area, the couple aroused no suspicion from the handful of tenants and building staff they encountered. They more than looked the part.

Rigging one of the canisters to the blower of the air-conditioning system took the better part of an hour for the expert terrorist team. It was energy efficient, well sealed, and constantly circulating clean air. The building was effectively circulating the deadly bacteria, leaving no suite uninfected. It would take three days for the tenants to become seriously ill, at least another day for tests to be run on those who talked to their doctors, but by the time the plague could be positively identified, some of the richest and most influential men and women in the world would be long dead.

It was a scenario already successfully enacted in several other countries. The incidents had been well executed, and those who had paid the ransoms had been warned not to alert the news media. Their silence could be counted on, and this new mission also would take place without a problem.

When the man had finished wiring the air ducts, the woman used a cell phone to call the Middle East. She spoke briefly in Arabic, then turned off the phone and helped finish the job. On the way out the front lobby, they informed the security guard that the leasing agent was having some problems and had asked them to alert him to go up with a key and a blanket. The request puzzled the man, but not the hundred-dollar tip he was handed.

Twenty-four hours later, in response to a series of messages sent simultaneously by Internet, fax, and courier, Spencer Cardwell and the city of Chicago authorized the wire transfer of fifty million dollars to a Middle Eastern bank known for its ties with Hamas. When the transfer was confirmed, information concerning the exact nature of the plague virus, as well as the appropriate antibiotic protocol for the cure, would be provided.

∽

The suspicious movements were detected first by satellite as subtle shifts along Korea's 38th parallel, the most heavily fortified border in the world.

For months there had been mounting rumors about possible war. The North Korean government had failed once again to halt the extensive famine devastating the country. Rumblings among the military increased political unrest and spontaneous uprisings against the government in the countryside.

It had been known for some time that North Korea was quietly making alliances with terrorist groups in Germany, Japan, and the Middle East. Some of these groups were connected with governments such as Libya and operated freely and openly. Others were intent on destabilizing their host nations in the hope of bringing down opposing governments.

But the ultimate goal was the same—to dramatically change the political face of Europe, Asia, and the Middle East, isolate the United States, turning it into a second-rate power, and then attack from both within and without.

A war in Korea would force the United States to reinforce South Korea when its forces would be stretched to their limits in the Middle East and other hot spots. War would bring Chinese troops to the Korean Peninsula just when the United States assumed old hostilities with the Communist regime had been defused through increased economic ties. Military, financial, and economic interests would eventually bring Japan into conflict as well as several of her trading partners. Additionally, other countries, including members of the European Union whose energy needs forged unexpected alliances in Jordan, Kuwait, Iran, Egypt, and elsewhere, would suddenly find themselves at political odds over the conflict.

Meanwhile, hit squads and "moles" trained in urban sabotage were being identified in the United States and among its allies. Men and women who had immigrated, taken jobs, married, and raised children, were seemingly assimilated into their new national identities. Yet, unknown to all but a handful of trusted contacts, they had positioned themselves to unleash biological weapons, sabotage government buildings, and disrupt transportation and communication centers. The movement toward armed confrontation between North and South Korea was the trigger that would unleash terrorist acts across the Western world.

Despite urgent intelligence warnings about the unfolding crisis, United States officials at first hoped that North Korea would exchange food and other humanitarian assistance for peace. A United Nations task force assessed the needs of the people, and approached member countries with requests for grain, medical supplies, and other essential relief. Private agencies, quietly active for years, were encouraged to step up their efforts. It was then that the UN decided none of the supplies it had gathered would be released until the North Korean government renounced the warlike stance it had taken for more than two generations. It was blackmail, pure and simple, but the UN also saw it as a means to an end.

The anticipated change, however, occurred very differently from what was originally expected. Rather than peace, North Korean leaders seemed determined to unite the people in war. Long suspected of having tactical nuclear missiles, the North was also known to have biological weapons that had been in readiness for years. Both the North and South had elite troops facing off at the border, with the North possessing a far superior army to launch a surprise attack. Thousands would die on the first day of such an assault, enough for the North to gain quick victory.

The no-man's-land between the opposing forces was thick with mines and other deadly traps and there was an atmosphere of constant saber rattling, especially when the North held joint military exercises with the widely deployed Chinese troops. But saber rattling was something quite different from what the satellites were now detecting. The situation along the 38th parallel was a major tactical shift, though its meaning was far from clear. Intelligence officers had intercepted rumors of shifting global alliances. Both Iraq and Iran had sent emissaries to Korea, officially for discussions related to oil and other resources that affected the North's economy. Unofficially, there were constant references to the old Arab maxim: "The enemy of my enemy is my friend."

If North Korea was going to launch an assault, it would likely come from three distinctly different zones. Yet the nature of the defensive troops already in place suggested something quite different. They would either have to wait for a first strike or initiate the violence that everyone had for so long feared.

An equally unsettling development came when several Middle Eastern leaders met secretly to consider a multi-front alliance, launching an assault against Israel while their new allies within North Korea made a simultaneous attack to the south. American and United Nations troops would be spread so thin their defeat was virtually guaranteed.

Chapter 2

EDNA WILLIAMS'S NEIGHBORHOOD was never visited by the tourist buses that cruised the theater district of Broadway, the newly refurbished Times Square, the Upper East Side museums, or the waterfront with its glorious view of the Statue of Liberty and Roosevelt Island. Near what had once been called Hell's Kitchen, in the Lower East Side's garment district, a stop-off point for junkies, gang members, and graffiti "artists," it was hardly Manhattan's pride and joy. The streets were a war zone. A war for human souls; a war in which too many young people had already fallen victim.

In the fifteen years Edna Williams had lived in her small one-bedroom, third-floor walk-up, she had witnessed countless murders, overdosed junkies, prostitutes abused by their pimps. Anyone who could had moved away and the rest lived alone and lonely like Edna. College students who disdained the dormitory life; workers sharing space while trying to rise above minimum wage; and an assortment of illegal aliens, street people, and misfits completed the scene.

Helen Hannah, Edna's granddaughter, had hated the idea of her grandmother taking the apartment, even when the area had still been classed only as "disreputable." She calmed her fears by telling herself that Grandmother Edna was a vibrant, active woman who had single-handedly raised not only her own four children, but grandchildren as well. Helen's aunts and uncle had long ago made lives for themselves far away, marriage and family taking them to Seattle, Montreal, and London. Only her mother had stayed behind, marrying a rising young attorney and moving into an airy, three-bedroom apartment in the East 80s. They had lived a good life, at least until that fateful day they left their children in the care of Edna, got on a plane, and flew to London to visit Aunt Charlotte.

No one could ever tell Helen what happened to her parents' plane. A bomb, mechanical failure, a stolen missile fired by a terrorist—all were theories that had been offered. Nothing was proven. Nothing was ruled out. All that was certain was that 237 people had perished, leaving behind loved ones who had struggled to understand.

Edna Williams stayed in her daughter and son-in-law's apartment, using the airline's settlement money to raise and educate her grandchildren. They attended parochial schools, eastern colleges, and eventually started careers; Helen becoming a high-profile news reporter, then anchor for the local station—WNN Television. What she hadn't realized until her grandmother moved was that Edna had no real resources of her own. The settlement had been substantial, and there had been insurance from her son-in-law's law firm, but it was all designated for the children. She made certain they had everything they needed to become a success, only allowing herself the luxury of a television and a VCR to watch the videotapes her pastor recommended to his congregation.

Helen had tried to help her financially as a way of saying thanks, not knowing if any other family members did the same. They all had very different lives and she knew her grandmother would have treated them all the same, no matter what they did or didn't do.

What she couldn't know was that her grandmother rarely used the money Helen gave her for herself. Shiata, for example, was a prostitute Edna had watched nightly from the street corner near her building. Befriending the young woman, barely out of her teens, she bought her coffee, talked with her, and shared child-raising tips when she discovered the girl had a little boy to support. Occasionally she convinced Shiata to join her at church, never telling anyone what the woman did to survive, never doing anything more than sharing God's love.

Edna finally convinced the girl to leave her broken life, finding her a small attic apartment in the home of a church member and helping her get by while earning a high school equivalency degree and becoming a cosmetologist. Shiata had eventually earned enough to begin paying for courses at City College, working toward a degree as a social worker.

Edna never talked about the girl or told anyone what

she was doing. Occasionally, Helen would find Shiata's little boy at her grandmother's on those days when his mother rushed directly from the beauty shop to one of her classes. She talked briefly with Shiata when the two women happened to meet in the building. But as far as Helen knew, she was simply one of her grandmother's friends from church and that was all she needed to know. The past was over, Edna Williams told Shiata. Jesus never condemned what you were. He just helped you to move on.

There were others as well. Pastor Holmes sometimes laughed about the "Bank of Edna Williams" when lecturing to the elderly woman about the street people she was always trying to help. "You can't support the world, Sister Edna," he'd say. "You can't love all of humanity."

"The Lord has provided for my needs," she would reply. "I have good friends who will never let me starve. But you're wrong about changing the world, Pastor Holmes. Don't you think I can help just two people turn from their path and find a life that is right with God?"

"Of course I do," the minister said and laughed.

"If you or I, or anyone can change just two people in their own lifetime," Edna persisted, "don't you think they could influence two more people for good?"

"That's a reasonable assumption," the pastor replied, not quite certain where she was leading him.

Edna smiled triumphantly. "Then you don't have to go very far before everyone on earth has a chance to change. We each affect just two lives for the better and pretty soon the entire world, billions and billions of people, have given their lives to Jesus."

"You're talking about the thousand-year reign of Jesus following Armageddon, aren't you?" asked the pastor thoughtfully.

"It doesn't matter what it's called," responded Edna. "I'm not even sure it matters what comes before as long as it's in God's hands. But I truly believe that if each of us tells the story to two others, tells it with the Holy Spirit's guidance, His kingdom will truly rule."

Walking the streets at all hours, befriending the friendless, Edna was scoffed at, ridiculed, and taunted. But she was also embraced and loved, even by those who thought she was just a crazy old lady with strange ideas, which was why she never moved, not even when Helen offered to buy her grandmother an uptown condominium near her own. "This is where the Lord has put me," Edna insisted. "This is where I do my work. When He is ready to take me home, I'll go joyously. Until then, try to see my neighbors as I do."

Helen would visit as often as she could, and called her grandmother two or three times a week. Worrying about the old woman's safety, yet also somehow realizing such concerns were unnecessary.

It was a typical Tuesday night when Helen Hannah called her grandmother a few minutes after the WNN Evening News signed off the air. "What a wonderful newscast you had tonight, Helen," said her grandmother.

"Wonderful? Grandmother," she replied. "We ran stories

about riots in the Golan Heights, violence between families of Holocaust survivors and the Ku Klux Klan in Skokie, Illinois. There was a flood in Nevada, an uprising by the generals in China, and the torture trial of General—"

"Yes. Yes. I saw it all," the old woman interrupted. "Tragedy in Europe. Tragedy in the Middle East. Tragedy in the United States. Tragedy everywhere. It's a time of trial for many people. I hope you and your crew remembered to pray for the folks you're reporting on."

"Grandmother," Helen said patiently. "I know how your faith sustained you when Mom and Dad died and you had to raise us kids, and I know how you live your life with faith. But have you been buying some of those 'happy pills' they sell on your street? The world is going to hell these days. In my television journalism classes, the professors used to joke about how 'if it bleeds, it leads.' We're taught to look for something visually horrible—a shooting, a riot, a plane crash site—and hook the viewer with it. Then you put a piece of happy news at the end so hopefully the viewer will tune in the next night." She sighed. "Do you know what our 'happy news' choices were for tonight? A war in the Balkans where only thirty people died compared with one hundred the day before, or a plane crash in Paris where a cat and two dogs were found alive in the smoldering wreckage. Everything else was war, threats of war, famine, earthquakes, plague, and, of course, bad hair days for half the movie stars in Hollywood . . ."

"You're teasing me, dear," her grandmother replied.

"But I'm serious. Remember what I've been telling you about our Bible study of the end times. Yes, the world is a mess, but that is just to let us see the hand of God in our lives. The worse your news broadcasts, the closer we get to Jesus. Sometime soon, any day now, in fact, there will be a rapture of the saved. After that, whoever is left behind at your network can report on the greatest story since the birth of our Savior."

"I wish I had your faith, Grandmother," was Helen's retort. "Every century there are people who predict the end times. A new millennium just brings out more of them. Do you know how many calls our network gets from people announcing the end of the world? The second coming of Jesus? The imminent landing of UFO's or the takeover of the White House by little green men from Mars? Maybe not all of them are crazy, but I don't think even you could tell which ones among them have a vision of the future and which ones are psychopaths."

"It's not what people say," Edna insisted. "It's what's in the Bible. From Daniel to Revelation, we're shown God's plan. I am sad for those who suffer, but the more our times reflect what is written, the closer we come to His return."

"We've been through this before, Grandmother," said Helen, trying to hide her annoyance. "I suppose I believe in God. I suppose I even believe in Jesus. But I also know without question that my parents were good people and I needed them desperately. I needed their love. I needed their wisdom and they were taken from us."

"And all you got was this old lady," Edna responded, her feelings hurt.

"No, that's not it, Grandma," countered Helen. "You couldn't have loved me more. Now that I'm older, I think I even understand how if you hadn't been a wonderful mother to Mom, she couldn't have been so wonderful to me. But I also know that I would have had your love whether Mom and Dad had lived or died. I wanted you all, Grandma. I wanted them *and* you. Sometimes, even now, I cry myself to sleep, questioning how God can exist and still allow such a tragedy. And then . . . And then I just hurt so much I don't know what to believe."

"I know. I really do understand," Edna interjected softly. "And despite your questioning, God understands too. Your mom was my daughter, and I loved your father like a son. There is no greater pain a parent can bear than the loss of a child. I expected your mother to bury me, not the other way around. I wanted her to grieve for me as I grieved for my mother, and she grieved for her mother before her. That is the natural way. And yes, I, too, was angry with God. I would have taken her place if I could have. Instead, I have to wait out my years here before going to be with them. But until then, you and I just have to accept His plans for us, to remember that ultimately He is in control."

"Does that really bring you comfort, Grandma?" Helen asked intently. "Is that how you found hope in tonight's newscast?"

"It truly is, Helen," Edna answered. "And one day it will

help you find hope, too. Why else would we want to carry on if not to fulfill His plan for our lives? You just watch. What is happening today in our lives, in the stories your network is covering, is unique in human existence. It is only a matter of time."

Chapter 3

BRONSON PEARL KNEW he was going to have a problem when the flight attendant asked him to remain on board as the other passengers disembarked. He'd already been through customs in England, where he'd been on assignment for WNN, before boarding the flight back to the States. Helen Hannah was supposed to be waiting for him in the parking area, so what was the problem, and why was the flight attendant keeping him longer than the old man in the wheelchair and the little girl flying alone to meet her parents?

The pilot finally opened the cockpit door and said, "Okay, Shirley. They're in place." Turning toward Bronson, he held up a copy of *Time* magazine. "Great picture of you on the cover, Mr. Pearl," he said. "Nice having you on board."

And then he knew. Helen had done it. Helen had really done it.

Bracing himself, Bronson Pearl left the plane and started up the ramp. He could hear them before he could see them, a half dozen WNN staffers, each with a different toy instrument. There was Chet, the intern from the news department, with a tiny trumpet in his large hands. There was Linda, the receptionist, on harmonica. Gareth, a newly hired sports reporter, had a toy piano, and Imogene, one of Helen's researchers, played a miniature saxophone. Ian, from advertising, held a kazoo, and Afi, the new hire in public relations, jammed with a tissue and a comb.

The music was off key, but recognizable; the theme from the "Bronson Pearl Report" on WNN, his weekly broadcast commentary.

He looked for Helen, not certain if he wanted to kiss or strangle her. For years he had half-joked about his lack of success. He had been featured on the cover of *TV Guide* and on the inside pages of *People* magazine. *Broadcast* magazine had done an article on how he'd been able to gain the trust of so many key world leaders. His salary had increased to the point where, if he really wanted he could retire and spend his days fishing up in the Pacific Northwest as he claimed he'd always wanted to do.

Not that Bronson Pearl had ever fished in his life. But he had once done a story about fishermen, average people who relaxed with a line in the water on a warm summer's morning. It seemed an idyllic life, and he'd often vowed to spend his retirement years doing nothing else.

Yet deep down Bronson knew he would never live out his fantasy. He loved his work regardless of the unwanted attention it brought him, and he'd finally adjusted to being a cable network star. "But I would like theme music," he'd said with a laugh.

"Theme music?" Helen had echoed. They had eaten at a posh restaurant in Lower Manhattan and were strolling back to her apartment on a balmy summer night.

"Theme music," he repeated. "Haven't you ever noticed the shows where, every time the good guy goes into action, you hear music? That's what I want. Theme music that plays everywhere I go. Now that would be real success."

Helen had laughed. "Bronson, you're crazy."

"Maybe," he replied. "But you can't tell me you haven't fantasized about your own theme music."

"Okay, Bronson," she sighed, with a smile. "The day you get your picture on the cover of *Time* magazine, I'll get you some theme music."

That had been months ago, one of those times too many stories of man's inhumanity to man had left them both exhausted, a moment of silliness that Bronson now remembered with chagrin.

The makeshift band moved behind Bronson as he walked from the arrival lounge. They matched his step, saying nothing, ignoring the stares of other passengers, tooting and honking for all they were worth.

"Helen . . . ," said Bronson, with mock anger. "Where are you?"

It was then he saw the poster at a newsstand. *Time* magazine's cover for the current week, with the headline "Bronson Pearl: The World's Most Trusted Newsman."

Helen Hannah stepped from behind it holding a piece of paper, a pencil, and a grin of delight in his embarrassment.

"Look . . . Over there!" she shouted, attracting the attention of passing passengers. "The man with the theme music. I'd know him anywhere. I've got to have his autograph!"

"Helen, I'm going to kill you," hissed Bronson as she rushed to his side. "I'm going to marry you and then I'm going to kill you."

Helen ignored him. Grinning broadly, she continued loudly, "I'm your biggest fan, Mr. Pearl!" Bronson kept walking, his face flushed, as his coworkers from WNN tagged along, playing his theme over and over

As they passed one of the bars, a rather large man, who'd apparently had a few too many in the airport lounge, moved unsteadily off his stool and stepped in front of Bronson. "I've been watching you, Pearl," he said angrily. "You celebrity types are so rude. Why don't you give the lady your autograph?"

Helen handed him the paper, trying to keep from laughing as the stranger watched him scribble his name.

"Can't you say something personal to the lady?" the man insisted, his breath sour and his eyes bloodshot.

"How about 'to my greatest fan, a beautiful and gracious lady'?" replied the exasperated Bronson. "That make you happy?"

The man nodded. Helen burst into laughter. The rest of the WNN crew managed to continue playing, more out of tune than ever.

"I owe you," said Bronson.

"I'm looking forward to it, Bronson," she quipped, then

smiled. *"Time* magazine . . ."* She looked at him for a moment, then kissed him tenderly. "I'm so proud of you," she whispered.

Bronson smiled, lost for a moment in her eyes, then looked back at the spectacle behind them. "Helen," he pleaded, "could we get out of here? I've never felt so foolish in my life."

Helen stopped, her face assuming a hurt, hangdog expression. "What's the matter, Bronson?" she whimpered, then burst into laughter. "Don't you like your theme?"

༄

They called themselves Women Who Witness, Arab and Israeli, Christian, Jew, and Muslim, most in their thirties and forties, but a few were barely out of their teens and among them, a few widows. Some were much older, having lost not only husbands and sons but also grandsons. Some followed traditions dating back thousands of years while others were totally contemporary. But they all wore the same modest head and body covering serving as both a gesture of respect for their orthodox Islamic members and as a way to conceal their identity.

They could be found as silent witnesses in the midst of a riot or a war zone, a reminder, they said, that there are no winners in such conflicts. Violence always means a grieving mother, wife, or daughter. To kill because of where someone was born or because of the language they speak, or because of how they worship the Creator is an abomination. The women said they were militant in their love, lifting their voices in prayer and song, each speaking in her native tongue—Hebrew, Arabic, English, Russian, or any of a dozen other languages. "God hears all," they claimed. "God understands all." They spoke out angrily against the atrocities in their midst, sharing their personal tragedies and taking a stand not as a buffer between opposing forces but as prophets who put their own lives on the line for the sake of the truth, their very presence articulating the senseless horror of war.

Initially the news media treated them as just a novel photo opportunity, striking figures amid the masked youths hurling stones and the police firing rubber bullets into hostile mobs. They were not generals or kings, presidents or religious leaders, and although some had attended college and graduate school, others could barely read or write. None of the women sought personal glory, never using their real names. They traveled along using routes that constantly changed, depending on a network of sympathizers, safe houses, and disguises. To do otherwise was to risk arrest and torture, putting at risk those who did not know a spouse or daughter who was a Women Who Witnessed.

The names they gave to the press and the authorities were those of historic women who had obeyed God and changed the world. One called herself Miriam; another, Sarah; a third, Elizabeth. There was a Hannah, a Mary, a Salome, a Eunice, and many others. Each was a reminder of a biblical event, an account of God's faithfulness unto death and beyond. Each namesake had endured difficult times: Sarah had been barren; Mary a humble Jewish teenager with a unique destiny; Eunice, the Jewish wife of a Greek and mother of Timothy in the early Christian church.

The witnesses had come together by chance—each having lost a son, a husband, a brother, or a father in the senseless violence that was spreading throughout the Middle East. They met in marketplaces and hospitals, synagogues, mosques, and churches, sharing their stories, as if guided by the hand of God, with women who were officially considered enemies. Each saw in the grief-stricken faces a mirror of her own soul. They gradually accomplished the "impossible," uniting in love, bonding in shared experience, and transcending the superficial differences that once had kept them apart.

In grief they became the sisters of Eve, whose son, Abel, was murdered through the greed, jealousy, and anger of his brother. In grief they became the sisters of Mary, whose son was killed on the cross in fulfillment of prophecy. They had not failed to see God's hand in such sorrows. They knew all was done according to His purpose, but they were mothers first, and mothers grieve the loss of even a wayward child. Their tears formed a communion that predated written history and would continue as long as man turned his back on God.

Early members of Women Who Witness also identified with Mary Magdalene; Mary, mother of James; and Salome,

who had discovered the empty tomb of Jesus. They were the
bearers of sorrow, but also the harbingers of the Good News,
challenging the evil that seemed to be overwhelming the
Middle East.

Women Who Witness first appeared in Jerusalem, at
the endlessly disputed site of the Temple Mount, contested
by followers of Judaism, Christianity, and Islam. Many
believed that God had once been physically present there
and would return there to rule the earth. Yet in His absence,
men had defiled the holy place by killing each other in His
name. And so the women stood in silent prayer while rubber bullets, rocks, and tear gas exploded all around.

It was Franco Macalousso who first sensed the potential
international influence of Women Who Witness. It was
impossible not to be stirred to compassion by their sincere
desire for peace, and even though they spoke of different
holy books and were of diverse faiths, they were not committed to any one teaching. By being inclusive, they no
longer felt themselves to be Christian, Jew, or Muslim.
They were determined to abolish divisiveness in spiritual
creeds.

Macalousso had begun meeting with the women, gaining their trust as he revealed his own plans for world peace.
Flattered by his attention, they were impressed that someone as well known and respected as he should take the time
to listen to them. While they knew little of his history, little
of his life, what mattered to them was that he had cared
about their cause. When they gave him their support, they

felt they were endorsing a man who understood the need for peace at any price.

In time, the presence of the Women Who Witness became a bigger story than the riots and terrorist attacks that drew them to trouble spots throughout the Middle East. With no political message, they claimed they would follow anyone who brought peace to the region, regardless of religious affiliation or nationality. "We would probably climb into bed with the devil if it would keep our children from dying in this senseless conflict," one of them had commented, a chilling statement to their detractors but equally uplifting to their supporters.

It was Bronson Pearl who covered the story of the Women Who Witness for WNN. A tragic and hopeful story that seemed to shine like a beacon of light in one of the darker corners of the world.

Pearl noticed early on how a questioning world was beginning to listen closely to the testimonies of the Women Who Witness. Interviewing the average man and woman on the street, they told him that they felt as if they were hearing their own lives resounding in the stories of the Women Who Witness. And they were especially responsive when the women began to question the values of government leaders, the military, even those spiritual heads who seemed to justify destruction with God's name.

Individuals who had not experienced the losses of the Women Who Witness began aggressively challenging their religious leaders, especially questioning Christians as to why the Creator was honored by the death of His Son. As car bombs and suicide missions, sniper fire and commando raids turned the Holy Land red with blood, these men and women began organizing local demonstrations to stand between violent factions. Often acting against the traditions of their culture, they faced angry family members, risking scorn, arrest, and even floggings as the Middle East continued rapidly spinning out of control. Leaders shifted armies, stockpiled weapons of mass destruction, and called upon allies to support a growing international military presence. Someone eventually had to say "no," and the Women Who Witness was the one force that best understood what was at stake. Or so the world had come to believe.

Bronson, however, remained skeptical. "Something's wrong with all this," he told Helen as they ate by candlelight the night of his arrival. "Remember when we were in Ireland a few years ago, covering the women's march for peace? They were a mix of Catholics and Protestants, but they were brought together by their religious faith, not just their anguish at the bombings and shootings. They had lost friends and loved ones too. There were widows and mothers who had lost children. Yet there was something different about them. Something . . ."

"Spiritual, Bronson?" Helen suggested.

"Yes," he agreed. "Like your grandmother. It's not that the Women Who Witness aren't sincere. It's just that they're like those one-issue politicians in the States. I get the feeling that they would tolerate a Hitler if he promised peace."

"You're getting cynical, my love," Helen warned. "Though I must admit that my grandmother agrees with you. She doesn't even like that UN consultant you interviewed."

"Macalousso?" replied Bronson. "At least his connection is understandable. He comes from the business world, and only weapons manufacturers think that wars are good for business. He's being courted by the European Union to take a high-profile post, and what's an alliance like that if not about business?"

"So," pressed Helen, "why are you covering Women Who Witness on the next Bronson Pearl Special?"

"I'm pragmatic too," he replied. "There are going to be specials on CBS, the BBC, CBC, CNN, and all the rest. I can do a report first—and hopefully better—or I could go back to reading the farm report at 2:00 A.M."

"You?" she joked. "The man who has won more industry awards than any broadcaster at the network?"

"I do this work because I get to be with you," Bronson replied sincerely. "Until you decide to retire and take up crocheting, I have to work at WNN or we'd never have time together. Besides," he concluded, "this is a real story, even if it makes me uncomfortable. If these women can ease the tensions in the Middle East, who am I to say they don't deserve coverage?"

Chapter 4

HELEN HANNAH'S REPUTATION as one of WNN's most popular news anchors was not as surprising as the fact that she had settled into a job long enough to be a success. Originally majoring in sciences, her early career plans focused on biomechanical research, but her inquiring mind led her to take additional classes in anthropology, history, and art and eventually her adviser suggested a switch to journalism. "You have the most curious mind I've ever encountered," he told her. "Everything in life excites you, and journalism is the one profession I know where you can get paid for being nosy."

Helen was embarrassed to tell her grandmother about her career change. Helen knew Edna had wanted her to find a job where she could help others and do good works. She had made a point of introducing her granddaughter to women making careers in ministry as educators, choir directors, missionaries, and ministers. She had often heard Pastor Holmes speak out against the media, criticizing the lack of moral fiber among reporters who would embarrass a

government official, but rarely attack an unethical busi-
nessman. The self-interest of advertisers and the bias of the
network owners interfered with journalistic objectivity.

But to Helen's surprise, Edna had enthusiastically sup-
ported her granddaughter's new interest. "Of course I'm
angered by what I read in the papers and see on television,"
she admitted. "But that doesn't mean there is anything
wrong with the media. The scrolls used to make the Bible
were the media of their day. And Jesus' disciple Luke was
like you. His first interest was science. He was a physician,
and he became a writer with two of his books in the New
Testament. The good Lord gave us free will, Helen. If you
are right before Him, it doesn't matter how you earn your
living."

Helen wasn't sure she shared her grandmother's faith.
She knew she loved God, but she was not sure she liked
Him. If the story was true, He had let His own Son die, and
He had certainly allowed her parents' deaths. She wasn't
sure what the media and God had in common, but she
cared very much that her grandmother approve of her new
profession. She just did not tell her of all the hypocrisy in
the name of news, because what was more important to
her was the growing sense of control that came with the
territory. As her success grew, she would decide who to
interview and what footage to shoot and broadcast. She
shaped the truth by whom she interviewed, the questions
she asked, and sometimes the questions she didn't ask. She
was fascinated with the morality of each choice she could

make. Editing meant power. Being in production meant power. Being the person on camera, interpreting the news, meant power.

Maybe she could not bring her parents back to life, or restore youth to the old woman who had raised her with such love and devotion. But she could produce something structured to her exact requirements and that made it all worthwhile. She was being "paid to be nosy," and she realized she could not have asked for a better job.

If there was any problem in her life, it was Bronson. Love meant giving up control, being vulnerable, and that was a pain she had already experienced. She remembered when her parents died and Pastor Holmes had talked about death being another part of life. She had not found his words particularly comforting. Maybe when she was older she'd share such a faith, she told herself, but for now she could feel nothing. As an adult, that feeling lingered, and she was afraid of getting involved with a man only to have him taken away from her as her parents had been.

It was easier to stay focused on work; the dangers the world was facing were unlike any that had ever been recorded. The Los Angeles earthquake had triggered even worse catastrophes: a volcanic eruption in Hawaii, a tidal wave off the coast of Japan, and a looming crisis in key agricultural regions due to unexpected climate changes. WNN reporters were always on the scene, providing twenty-four-hour coverage of the growing terrorist activities that had led the European Union, the United Nations, the

U.S. government, and a host of other countries and organizations to begin redeploying their military personnel. Rapid deployment forces were being heavily reinforced. America had quietly reinstated the draft, and National Guard units were being mobilized for retraining to fight in one or another global hot spot. There were violence and despair as war forced people to evacuate their homes, leave their jobs, and journey to refugee camps. Occasionally, individual acts of heroism and compassion revealing the triumph of the human spirit in these dark days made the evening news, brought live to the world by Helen and her team.

∽

For those whose job it was to analyze world events, the developments in the Middle East were baffling. Astute observers saw multinational troops being drawn into a series of conflicts increasingly focused on the area of Megiddo. Alliances formed months or years earlier—based on oil, food, or weapons—were suddenly called into play. Russian, American, French, German, Chinese, Syrian, Lebanese, Jordanian, Iraqi, and Iranian troops were deploying in an ever-tightening knot around Israel. Missiles were being retargeted, nuclear and biological weapons were being quietly placed atop warheads, and conventional troops were being positioned for maximum first-strike capability. Former enemies were acting in consort while former friends found themselves in conflicting alliance, and yet no

single issue seemed urgent enough to warrant these increasingly dangerous power plays.

"The world has become an elementary school playground where immature children are playing a dangerous
game of chicken," commented Hogarth Chapman, commentator on WNN's Evening News. A former official with
the U.S. State Department, he had wide experience in
global confrontation. A college student during the Suez
Canal Crisis, he had witnessed the Berlin Airlift, the Cuban
Missile scare, the rising tensions between India and
Pakistan, and the rise of the Islamic fundamentalists in
Iran.

"The weapons of mass destruction have changed,"
Chapman's commentary continued. "The bombs dropped
on Hiroshima and Nagasaki evoked a fear that lasted for two
generations, yet their destructive force was not even as great
as the firestorm bombing of Dresden in World War II."

"We 'refined' our thermonuclear weapons during the
Cold War, making them bigger and more powerful, able to
destroy entire cities or to eradicate whole armies in seconds.
Although the major powers quickly amassed large atomic
arsenals, they also controlled the means of production, pre-
venting other nations from gaining such power. Yet small
countries surrounded by enemies, such as Israel and
Pakistan, used spies, double agents, bribery, and theft to
acquire atomic secrets and equipment. Others, such as Iraq,
began developing their own weapons of mass destruction.
Anthrax, bubonic plague, and other deadly diseases were

obtained from legitimate research labs. Chemical weapons are even more widespread with countries such as Iraq possessing enough to kill every man, woman, and child in the world many times over. Such weapons are simpler, deadlier, and harder to stop than even the largest of thermonuclear bombs."

Helen Hannah, acting as the narrator for Chapman's alarming program, went on to explain that the emerging international crisis was one once considered impossible. The manufacture of such weapons was undertaken with the belief that they were too horrible to use.

"The statistics were chilling," she reported. "The United States alone has missiles targeted to sixteen thousand sites, mostly in the former Soviet Union. This was not our whole nuclear arsenal, just the number of missiles that can be launched simultaneously should war break out."

"Our deterrent policy involved our enemies knowing we were prepared to destroy them," added Hogarth Chapman. "But no one ever believed we would attempt such a launch. And even though we downsized at the end of the century, we still have the capacity to destroy the world."

Helen Hannah explained to the viewers what nuclear destruction would actually mean. "The long-term effect would be devastating," she asserted. "Radiation would poison water and crops throughout the earth. The necessities we need for life would become the means of our death. The detonations would create atmospheric changes that would reduce growing seasons and alter global temperatures, meaning colder weather and widespread famine. Hotter conditions would melt portions of the polar ice caps, causing oceans and rivers to rise, flooding fertile land essential to farmers. Epidemics of disease, mass starvation, and the collapse of civilization would destroy life as we know it."

"There is no precedent in world history for what is taking place in the region surrounding Megiddo," added former State Department envoy Melissa Hargrove, a commentator in WNN's radio division. "There is no monster bent on conquering the world, no Alexander the Great, no Attila the Hun, no hate-filled madman like Adolf Hitler. Past wars have always involved an enemy against which the good people could rally. This time there is no one against whom the nations of the world can focus. Will the nations of the earth back off, to say 'Enough'? God help us, but I fear that a war, in which all civilization will be the ultimate loser, has already begun."

Many people agreed with the dire warnings of the experts and that which seemed so certain would somehow come to pass. Others petitioned their government leaders, pleading for cool heads and reasoned judgment. While others, angered by what they were witnessing, demanded whatever force was necessary to restore order in the Middle East.

But a few, like Edna Williams, read their Bibles and went about their business, praising the Lord for each new development, even while having compassion for those who were suffering. "Let the time of trial be short, oh Lord," beseeched

Edna during her daily devotionals. "I see Your hand in all this suffering, but I can't help seeing the suffering as well. I accept that those who are in pain and sorrow will be comforted by the love of Your Son, who knows our human hurts. Just let me always remember the words our Lord Jesus spoke, 'Thy will, not Mine.'"

Chapter 5

"I MEANT WHAT I SAID AT THE AIRPORT," announced Bronson Pearl. He was sitting with Helen in the backseat of the plush limo the network had sent to bring him into the city. His eyes were closed, his left hand holding hers. It was the first time in days he had been able to truly relax. "About marrying you."

"It wouldn't do a thing for your ratings," Helen joked. "You might even lose your status as the most trusted man in broadcasting."

"You can't hide behind jokes all your life, Helen," Bronson chided. "I love you, and as much as you don't want to deal with the fact, you love me too. I want you for my wife. No matter how much time we spend together, it's not enough. No matter how devoted we feel to each other, it's not the same commitment as marriage."

"Bronson, I . . . ," Helen stammered.

"And don't tell me that the world is going to hell," cautioned Bronson, "that it's no time to be raising children or that our jobs are so consuming we'd never be happy. I've heard all your excuses and I know they're all evasions. Even your grandmother says so. The only thing wrong with you is that you're afraid of commitment."

"No, I'm not," protested Helen. "I'm just afraid of what commitment might bring."

"It's certainly not going to be the little suburban home with the picket fence, a dog, and 2.3 children," joked Bronson. "We're not that type. But love without marriage is hollow. It's a denial of what commitment truly means." He leaned in closer. "We're not kids, Helen. We've each got twenty years in this business, and we've both been through bad relationships. We've seen enough human tragedy to know that the good things in life don't last forever."

"That's the problem, Bronson," sighed Helen. "Everyone I've ever loved has let me down. As a little kid, my teachers taught me about the love of Jesus. Then my parents died, and when I tried reaching out to Jesus, all I could feel was emptiness."

"Your parents were killed in a plane crash," Bronson replied gently. "They didn't abandon you. They could neither have predicted what occurred nor prevented it. Everybody experiences pain and loss. And everybody questions God at some time in their lives. But that doesn't mean you have to be held back by the past. It's time to get over it."

Helen sighed. "I can't get over the feeling I've done something so terribly wrong that God's determined to keep me from being truly happy."

He paused, reaching out and touching her cheek.

"Helen, I'm Bronson Pearl, the most trusted journalist in America. *Time* magazine said so. I even have theme music. And I'm telling you I love you. I want to marry you and spend my life with you." He looked deeply in her eyes, never letting go of her hand. "Now," he asked again, "will you marry me?"

০১০

"Don't ask," said Helen Hannah as she entered the production department where work was under way on what WNN staffers were calling "The Macalousso Project." It was a rush-to-air biography of the newly elected president of the European Union, and it was being handled by Helen and Kathy Tamagachi, from the Special Projects Division of the station. Kathy was delighted with the assignment, but Helen was leery of Macalousso and his aims. She tried to tell herself she hadn't compromised, that the depth made the difference because the truth could finally be revealed. There might be many wars to fight in a career, but this was not one of them, she told herself, and at least she could work with Kathy, whose skills and integrity as a journalist she respected highly. She was considered a top producer and editor at network headquarters, which was why she was assigned to Helen. A true professional, her desk, equipped with multi-line phone, in-line recorders, and two computers, was covered with stacks of file folders. The editing bays, monitors, and related equipment that filled the rest of the room were constantly humming.

As a result the floor had become the sorting area for the footage being edited for the Franco Macalousso documentary. Stacked tapes and film cans had been gathered for weeks from all over the world, and while some editors in the news department wanted to take credit for anticipating the recent changes in world events, the truth was they had all been caught off guard. Franco Macalousso had come seemingly out of nowhere to become the most influential leader in the modern world. It was rumored he had previously contemplated some sort of religious life but abandoned it while in his early twenties. Records showed that he had made a fortune in the communications industry and had subsequently gone to work with the United Nations where his public rise to a position of global influence made him the natural choice for an in-depth broadcast biography.

Kathy was running a tape of Macalousso when Helen arrived with sandwiches, coleslaw, and coffee from a nearby deli. With time pressures mounting, they had begun working through lunch. "Don't say one word about Bronson Pearl to me," Helen warned her partner. "If you have any questions, you can ask him yourself."

"That serious, huh?" said Kathy, laughingly holding up her hands.

Helen scowled and got down to work. "Forgive my disrespect of Macalousso and the Women Who Witness." Helen frowned. "The way he's been courting them, it's like he's building a cult following," she said.

"My, you are cynical," replied Kathy, taking a bite from her sandwich.

Helen switched on the monitor speakers to hear the audio track Kathy had been assembling from Macalousso's United Nations appearances.

"I firmly believe that these women are the vanguard of those who understand what is required for the return of the Messiah," Macalousso was saying as he introduced the Women Who Witness during a press conference held prior to their appearance before the General Assembly. "The Middle East is a land where too many people look to the heavens for a peace only they can bring about. Many say that God holds the power of life and death, peace and war, justice and mercy. They claim God wants them to suffer, but if God's will is behind every rock thrown, every grenade exploded, every shot fired, it is not to the heavens we should be looking but to ourselves. It's our words that fan the flames of hatred between brothers and sisters. Our hands make the bombs and launch the rockets and fly the fighter planes. And mankind can do unspeakable violence while blaming some God in heaven, so he can bring about his own boundless joy. Only we can heal one another. Only we can nurture the weak and helpless. Women Who Witness understand that God is within each one of us. We are all gods. These anonymous women have chosen to accept the responsibility so many of us avoid. They have homes and families. They have tended the sick and the dying, nurtured the weak and helpless. They radiate the best of the God within and they stand as witnesses against those who would choose pain and suffering. It is fitting that they should have formed in the Holy Land, because their message is one that resonates around the world. They stand where the Messiah will stand; their witness will grace the pages of holy books yet to be written."

"How can you argue with that?" asked Kathy, looking up from the monitor.

Helen didn't reply, watching instead a series of interviews by a WNN field reporter who had taken several of the women aside at the United Nations. One of the women in the group, a Jew from Brooklyn, New York, seemed embarrassed by Macalousso's comments. "He sounds like one of those New Age motivational speakers," she remarked. "The ones that tell you good people deserve to be rich, that you don't need a college education or a good job, or an inheritance. Instead they tell you to embrace the God inside you, buy their tapes and books, and attend their seminars. And if you don't get rich, at least you know where your money went . . . into their pockets."

Another, a Christian, thought her Jewish friend was being too skeptical. "I think he meant that we are partners with God, not gods ourselves," she ventured. "Didn't the Lord give us free will? We all know that we can nurture His creation or we can destroy it. I think Macalousso's talking about personal responsibility as Jesus taught."

"It doesn't matter what he said or what he meant," interjected a third. "He's a very powerful man who has enabled us to maintain a witness to the world. We are all of different faiths, different backgrounds, but we stand together as sisters determined to bring about peace. If this man, who is not of my people, not of my religion, not of my culture, can end the violence that has brought us all such personal sorrow, I will follow him anywhere."

"A cult," snorted Helen as the tape concluded. "Next thing you know they'll be wearing uniforms. I still don't see what makes Macalousso so important that we should be putting this biography together. Bronson did a series on him when he joined the United Nations. It didn't seem like that big a deal then, and I don't see why it is now. He's been lucky with his peace initiatives, that's all. Sure, he's center stage in the world's crises, but maybe things will work out and Franco Macalousso will end up as next year's game show trivia question. So what makes him so important to WNN?"

"Besides the fact that he is one of our employers, Helen?" Kathy asked.

"Are you serious?" Helen gasped.

"Fifteen percent share in the company, at least," Kathy informed her. "And a whole lot of other properties that would surprise you. Macalousso's business days were *very* successful, with lots of straw businesses seemingly independent of Macalousso Enterprises, each with a stake in what he wanted to buy. Unless you spent weeks tracing the paper trail, you'd never know what he was up to."

"Is that legal?" asked Helen, surprised by how much she did not know about this man and his power.

"Just good business," replied Kathy. "You don't get to be a billionaire in communications by making mistakes that can get you in trouble. This is the guy who put together a powerful satellite network of third-rate independent television stations around the world. He's also the guy who funded development of a two-way miniature voice pager, the one that allows multinational companies to keep track of their employees no matter where they're traveling."

"And now he's president of the European Union," added Helen. "What's his next move going to be? Becoming pope?"

"He'd probably see being pope as a step to a higher calling." Kathy laughed. "He seems to thrive on a pace that would kill the average person."

"And now he's our boss," said Helen. "I hope you treat him nicely in the final cut of our documentary."

"It's not hard," Kathy replied. "But the weird part about him is that he never seems to age. In fact, all the sags and wrinkles he started to get years ago seem to have smoothed out recently."

"Plastic surgery?" ventured Helen, intrigued that Mr. Perfect might have a streak of vanity.

"I don't think so," replied Kathy. "This guy seems to thrive on work. I don't think he's got time for anything else. No wife or kids. Just a few billion dollars in the bank, and a leadership role in the United Nations, and Macalousso's efforts have been succeeding in ways no one could have hoped. But despite his accomplishments, almost nothing is known about his background. He was born in a small village and tutored by the local priest. He went to a seminary for a while, began drifting, taking odd jobs while attending several different colleges to study business, electronics, political science, and psychology. But he was never much of a student. You have to look at his career in hindsight to see how brilliant he's been all along. He took what no one else wanted, and linked it together into a global business. Macalousso Enterprises is run from Rome. But he has key people in every major city of the world. His communication network can reach three-fourths of the globe, and his investments in both the United States and the Third World have given him enormous political influence. The truth is, he could adversely affect the economies of more nations than anyone cares to admit."

"But doesn't the United Nations have rules about blind trusts and divestitures?" Helen asked.

"I think they wanted him to keep active in his businesses to maintain his economic influence," Kathy explained. "Certainly he's gotten the results they have wanted. I mean, who better than someone with a real economic stake in world peace and stability to lead them?" She paused and then continued, "But the really strange thing is how Macalousso suddenly went from being a minor-league player to a leading world figure. Most men would sell their souls for the success he's had in just one field. But he's done it over and over again. And now they're saying peace in the

Middle East is dependent solely upon his negotiating skills. It just doesn't make sense to me."

"It's not our problem," Helen interjected. "I've asked to have Bronson do the final interview with Macalousso to wrap up the documentary. It will be his job to get answers to those questions."

Chapter 6

F RANCO MACALOUSSO WAS ANGRY, an emotion he let
 few people ever see. Not even United Nations Special
Agent Len Parker, the man who worked as his assistant now
that Macalousso was president of the European Union, had
ever witnessed such rage. They both knew that anger,
appropriately directed, could be a strength, but it could also
show a weakness, revealing things that truly mattered and
thereby passing on knowledge to one's enemies.

To Parker, his boss's anger seemed misplaced. It was not
Bronson Pearl's fault that Macalousso's rise to power
sparked the interest of one of the world's most important television networks. Bronson Pearl was not the enemy. Len
Parker knew this interview was important, and its timing
would be crucial to Macalousso's master plan, a clarion call
for the fulfillment of his destiny. The words and images
Bronson Pearl and the WNN staff would broadcast to the
farthest reaches of the world would make him the most
familiar leader in history. The documentary would create
the myth of his life and calling, allowing him time to take

control before they at last knew the truth of who he was and with whom he had come.

But Macalousso felt as if he had waited long enough already. He wanted to be fully in control now, not dependent upon anyone else, especially a lowly TV journalist. To have come this far, from a peasant village to absolute control over the world's largest communication consortium and to hold the reins of power in the U.N. and the European Union . . . Why should he have to submit to a man like Bronson Pearl?

Macalousso took a deep breath then exhaled slowly. The window of his penthouse apartment overlooked a lush public garden where butterflies flitted among the blooming flowers and mothers strolled with their children. How different life would soon become for all of them.

Soon, certainly no later than a few days after the scheduled airing of the eagerly awaited WNN special, he would assume his rightful place in the world, taking on the power he lusted for and, finally, find peace from the anger that overwhelmed him.

ᴄᴧᴐ

"You didn't give him an answer?" Edna asked anxiously. She and her granddaughter were sipping coffee in a corner of the WNN commissary, when the subject of Bronson Pearl's proposal came up. "Bronson Pearl has been chasing you for three years. He finally decides it's time to make a commitment, and you don't immediately say yes? Helen

Hannah, I thought I raised you better than that. Don't you know what is important in life?"

"Marriage may not be possible for everyone," Helen said, setting down her coffee cup and taking her grandmother's hand. "You had a very special relationship with Grandfather. Few people are as lucky as you two were."

"Utter nonsense, young lady!" said the older woman, in an irate tone at her granddaughter's misunderstanding. "What your grandfather and I experienced was *normal*, the way all marriages should be and can be! Because you're afraid, you won't reach out to the joy that you deserve." Her voice softened. "I buried my daughter, Helen Hannah! She was your mother, yes. But she was also my child. I railed at God for that. I wept bitterly at the burden He had thrust upon me. What did He know about childcare and the stress of raising kids? Oh, I tell you, I gave the Lord a piece of my mind! And now I'm going to give one to you!" Helen sighed and braced herself. "Bronson Pearl finally got around to asking you to marry him and you let him go without an answer," her grandmother continued. "Did you tell him you're afraid of commitment? That you're afraid of joy? Did you tell him you're afraid to find love and happiness?"

"Not exactly," replied Helen hesitantly.

"What then?" Edna demanded. "It's not like you're on a mission devoting yourself to the starving people of some isolated jungle. You're a journalist and a very successful one. You've got to learn to open up and share your life. If Bronson finally got around to asking you to marry him, say yes."

Helen looked down at her coffee cup, deep in thought. "It isn't the first time he's asked me," she admitted. "Bronson told me there would be no one else for him six months after we met."

"I knew I liked that young man for something other than his looks," exclaimed her grandmother. She leaned forward intently. "Just say yes, Helen," she begged. "Trust me on this. I've been through this. I didn't always like your grandfather. We fought. He was stubborn. I was stubborn. But ultimately we worked through our differences. Ultimately we found compromise. Ultimately we kept going back to the love that is God's gift to us. That's what love can do for you. That's what commitment can do for you. That's why you're going right back to your office to tell Bronson Pearl you will marry him."

"He's gone, Grandmother," whispered Helen, tears welling in her eyes. "He's back in the Middle East, in a place called Megiddo. It looks like if there's going to be a war, Bronson will be right in the middle of it." She began to weep.

Edna stood up, walked around the table, and took her granddaughter in her arms. She held Helen against her chest as she wept deeply, oblivious to her surroundings, oblivious to anything other than her grandmother's comforting touch.

❧

The change at first was subtle. Sporadic gunfire had been heard for days, and with snipers, tactical units, and civilian patrols swarming the area, it was impossible to tell who was shooting at whom or why. Each armed group seemed to have staked out its own territory, targeting its enemies, digging into entrenched positions. Initially the gunfire had been mostly small arms—handguns, rifles, the occasional shotgun or even a hand grenade. Many civilians maintained such weapons, especially the Israelis, who were subject to instant call-up for full military duty.

But the sounds were now louder and deeper as higher-powered arms were brought to the front, including anti-tank weapons, machine guns, and shoulder-fired rocket launchers. The distant sounds of collapsing buildings attested to the escalation. Aircraft flew around the clock, the sky full of reconnaissance planes, armored helicopters, fighters, and bombers. Meant as a show of force, the aircraft engaged in dangerous games of aerial "chicken," resulting in fiery crashes throughout the region.

Journalists assigned to the area were prepared for every eventuality: injections to protect them against biological assault, gas masks, and bullet-resistant vests and helmets. Several had handguns in their tote bags, though most preferred to work unarmed, knowing that spies and assassins often pretended to be journalists, carrying counterfeit credentials from major networks. As a result, any journalist caught with a weapon was instantly suspect and marked for death, so only the inexperienced traveled with guns.

Bronson Pearl had flown directly to Israel following his interview with Franco Macalousso in Paris. The newsman was told the European Union president would next fly to the Middle East in order to continue his peace negotiations. It seemed likely, however, that an escalation into full-scale warfare would erupt before Macalousso could arrive on the scene.

Judith Shimowitz, the Tel Aviv–based videographer, had been assigned by WNN to accompany Bronson Pearl to an interview with Israeli general Moishe Alizar. It was conducted over a large table spread with maps showing the positions of dozens of different armies, totaling more than two million men and women. Of greatest concern to the general was a segment of Megiddo where the largest battle seemed likely to erupt, a section that allowed ground movement only through a narrow pass, centuries old and surrounded by water and mountains. The impending battle would depend entirely on the location of the opposing forces.

"General Alizar, to many of our American viewers, the name of the place where we are standing has deep significance," commented Bronson. "It is said that the final battle between good and evil will begin here in Armageddon."

"Is that what you believe, Mr. Pearl?" responded the general.

"I believe that when people are convinced that something is going to happen, they find a way to make their beliefs come true," the reporter replied. "If they believe that this is the start of a war to end all wars, then it may well come to pass."

"Such talk does not matter to me or the state of Israel,"

snapped the general. "I am a Jew and this is my land. For two thousand years we Jews have been a hated people. If we try to live among ourselves, raising our own food, making our own clothing, building our own homes, practicing our faith within our own territory, we are attacked. We have been declared blight on the face of the earth. Our land is coveted because we have made it productive. We have been despised, dispersed, and reviled for trying to live in harmony with our beliefs. We have been tortured and murdered, yet always God has been with us. He has reminded us that He is faithful, chastised us when we turned away from Him, and ultimately brought us into this land. It is a place of refuge, a place of opportunity, a reminder of what can happen if we keep faith with Him. We will fight because we can do nothing else. What we face is what we have always faced. The names change. The alliances are different. Yet always we have known that we must live as one and die as one."

"The history of your people and this land is a tragic one," agreed Bronson. "But isn't this situation somehow different? If one of the extremist groups in this area acts irresponsibly, it will be like a lit match to a fuse. A full-scale world war might start before cooler heads prevail."

"That is true, Mr. Pearl," agreed the general. "That is why our defense minister has insisted that journalists have unlimited access to the front. We are a people of the Torah. The early scribes wrote the Word of God, and you are an electronic scribe. What you report reaches billions. Your words, your insight, and the truth the Lord gives you may be the only hope we have. We generals know how to destroy. You have the capability of bringing the truth. It is a special gift and I know you have been honored for it. We will see how God uses it in the days ahead."

Chapter 7

THE DESIGNER OF THE WNN BROADCAST STUDIO had created what he called an "environment for the twenty-first century." Brushed-aluminum trim on the desks curved gracefully into a sculpture that was meant to mimic the anatomy of the human heart. "The newsroom is the heartbeat of your communication empire," he had explained in his initial proposal.

On the wall behind the anchor desk was a bank of monitors with satellite feeds from around the world, each labeled with the country of origin. And each reinforcing the idea that WNN provided breaking news worldwide, twenty-four hours a day, seven days a week. To Helen Hannah and the rest of the staff of WNN, this high-tech environment was their home.

Except Bronson. There had been a time when a live feed was enough for Helen to feel intimate with the man she loved, his voice transmitted through the tiny receiver, his image on a dozen monitors around the set. She could close her eyes and almost feel his touch. It was a false intimacy, and during his absences she had long used the network set to maintain that semblance of closeness.

But now he was far away in a place called Armageddon on an assignment that would keep them apart during the most tumultuous crisis the world had ever known.

It was 6:23 eastern time, and while the picture feed was being relayed, there was still no sound, no chance yet to speak to him. Instead, the director instructed Helen to switch to Yuri Breedlaff at the Pentagon, where Pentagon spokesperson Richard Stanfield was making an announcement.

"Mr. Stanfield," the reporter queried, "it is our understanding that the president and his family are boarding the aerial command center in anticipation of a possible first-strike nuclear attack against Washington, D.C. Is that true?"

"I must argue with your choice of words, Mr. Breedlaff," the spokesman responded. "As you well know, Air Force One is always a mobile command center. It is equipped with all the military codes and special equipment the president needs to conduct a war or run the country. There is nothing special about this particular trip."

"That is not what we're being told, Mr. Stanfield," the reporter persisted. "We've heard from well-placed sources within your own agency that key personnel are being evacuated to Colorado Springs."

"Colorado Springs has been a favorite vacation spot of the president since long before he entered politics," Stanfield shot back. "He travels there often."

"Except that it is not a vacation, is it?" Breedlaff probed.

"The president is not staying in any of the town's hotels, nor will he be visiting any of his friends. Our source tells us that he will be headquartered in the Strategic Air Command bunker created for his use during the Cold War. We have also determined that key members of Congress, the Senate, and his cabinet will be joining him."

"Are you deliberately trying to panic the American people?" demanded an angry Stanfield.

"Please answer the question, Mr. Stanfield," the reporter requested politely.

"I won't dignify it with an answer," the spokesman snapped back. "This interview is now over."

Helen appeared on the screen, sitting at the news desk. "Yuri?" she said. "What can you tell us about the president and his family at this present moment?"

"You just heard the official version, Helen," the reporter replied. "The president is on his way to Colorado Springs. There is, and I quote, 'Nothing special about this trip.' But members of Congress have also been confirmed to be among the presidential party. Our sources tell us that this is the start of an evacuation to assure the smooth running of the country should full-scale war break out. The situation is said to be extremely grave despite official denials."

"Thank you, Yuri," said Helen from the studio. "And for a frontline perspective, we bring you Bronson Pearl direct from Armageddon. Are you there, Bronson?" Her voice was calm and professional, betraying nothing of the inner turmoil she felt.

Bronson appeared on screen. "The situation becomes more tense by the moment, Helen," he reported. "A few minutes ago the violence began escalating. There are reports of troop movements, but we have not been able to determine who is on the move and preparing to dominate the territory."

"Will the war be limited to Armageddon, Bronson?" asked Helen tensely.

Bronson looked grim. "The generals have told me that if one country makes a serious power grab here in Israel, retaliation will be on a global basis. Cities have been targeted worldwide, and unless a miracle happens on this tiny strip of land, we could be seeing a conflict of unprecedented proportions."

As Helen broke for a commercial she signaled the engineer to keep Bronson's mike open. "Can't you get out of there?" she asked him.

"This is where the story is, Helen," he replied matter-of-factly.

"I don't care about the story," she shot back. "I care about you. You're in ground zero of a war zone."

He shook his head. "Helen, you're in a city that's as much a target as Megiddo, maybe more. This is our job. Whatever happens, we've got to witness it."

"You can't report a story if you're dead," she pleaded. "Bronson . . . I love you."

"Helen . . . ," he began.

Suddenly the picture began to shake and a loud noise broke into the satellite feed. Helen could see figures rushing around carrying gas masks, and the camera was set on the ground, still running, so that the operator could don her mask. Bronson was heard shouting something unintelligible and the picture went black as a violent explosion severed all connection with Armageddon.

"On in 5, 4, 3 . . ." The floor director signaled Helen that they were out of the commercial and were about to air footage of Franco Macalousso. Helen cleared her throat and read from the TelePrompter.

"In Rome, European Union President Franco Macalousso announced his departure for the Middle East in a last-minute attempt to defuse the situation. Macalousso has been instrumental in negotiating previous settlements among warring factions in Eastern Europe." Helen's voice caught, the last images of Bronson swimming in her mind. Something was happening. Something serious. She wanted to scream, cry, run to the engineers and see if they could restore contact to Armageddon. But she had to stay calm and be professional.

She found herself wishing she had said yes to Bronson Pearl. Her grandmother was right. What had she been waiting for? The end of the world?

∽

The aircraft was a light pleasure craft with no military value, propeller driven, slow flying, and unable to perform complex maneuvers, the perfect plane for this clandestine mission. The pilot, not yet eighteen, was the son of fanatical extremists who believed that neither Jews nor Christians nor Moslems were practicing the true will of God. His father was in jail for the bombing of a marketplace in East Jerusalem. One brother had been killed by an Israeli commando unit, another brother was in training in Libya, hoping to return as part of a suicide squad. His mother operated a safe house in Jerusalem, a hiding place for agents traveling to and from their missions. They all shared the conviction that God worked through violent change, and that they were instruments of God.

The bombs that had been loaded on the aircraft could be hand-dropped by the pilot. A remote control device would trigger the explosions a few hundred feet above Tel Aviv. The detonations would send deadly chemicals raining downward where wind currents would then carry them for several miles over the city, blanketing it with an invisible mist of death.

The pilot checked his fuel and his radio, Uzi machine pistol and a gas mask at his side. A small first-aid kit contained the antidote to the bombs' chemical payload. His plan was to land the plane after the mission and walk away through the devastation he had caused. Everything in readiness, he hit the ignition.

❧

Chung Kwan Wong was a military leader of the New China and a student of history who viewed himself carrying on the great tradition of the ancient emperors. For centuries the

Chinese had been at a technological disadvantage with their enemies, constantly overrun by invading armies, conquered, and enduring the violence of bloodthirsty tyrants. But the unity of Chinese society was due, in part, to the people's recognition of their unusual situation. Each time a conquering nation was repelled or overturned, the Chinese resumed the same legal and social system they had known for centuries. They kept their identity, never assimilating, biding their time until they could regain control of their vast territory.

The Chinese land mass and population, along with the unity of their society, had made them a global power, a giant finally roused to action after centuries of victimization.

Chung Kwan Wong understood all this, but he also understood that the perilous situation in the Middle East had given him and his fellow navy submarine officers a unique opportunity. If they could target a ship of one of the superpowers with the tactical nuclear weapon they had secretly loaded, they could trigger a conflict that would change history. The war Wong envisioned would destroy the United States, Britain, France, Russia, Germany, India, and most other powerful nations, and demoralization would prevent the survivors from continuing the battle. China, of course, would not escape the carnage, but their advantage lay in pure numbers. With major cities in China destroyed there would still be a billion people inhabiting the nation, a population seeking the leadership of young military officers—men like Wong, trained to understand the past, foresee the future, and act in the present.

It was 3:00 P.M. when Wong made his desperate move, ordering the loading of the tactical nuclear warhead as a "training exercise" and targeting an American troop ship with almost five thousand sailors on board. He joked with his men as the digital clock counted down to the firing. None of them knew he had changed the computer codes and that this time the launch was for real.

⌀

Franco Macalousso's plane touched down on a military landing strip. No throngs of admirers, no special escort, no reporters shouting questions greeted him. As he and two aides hurried to a waiting staff car, a converted four-wheel-drive vehicle, with the tires designed to stay inflated under attack and an undercarriage reinforced against land mines. The passenger compartment was built to sustain a direct hit from a tactical rocket. Nothing was going to stop the president of the European Union from reaching his objective.

⌀

Helen Hannah was resting on a small couch in the break room. Her newscast was over and the on-air staff was on twenty-four-hour alert. Most had gone home to their families. A few took hotel rooms close to the studio. Only Helen decided to stay, knowing that if Bronson Pearl was still alive, his most likely link to the States would be through WNN.

It was 2:30 in the morning when an engineer tapped her on the shoulder.

"Helen?" he said. "Helen?"

Helen murmured something barely intelligible as she woke up. She had not thought she could sleep until Bronson's whereabouts were known. Now, from the look on the engineer's face, she feared the worst.

"What is it?" she demanded. "Is it Bronson?"

"We've got the feed up again," he told her. "There was a sniper attack, but Bronson is fine. Look, he's on the line. Ask him yourself."

Helen rushed to a small broadcast booth where the engineer switched the satellite signal directly to a monitor.

"Bronson," she cried with relief. "What's happening?"

"Macalousso's here," he replied, "but I don't think he can do anything. I think only God can do anything now."

"What do you mean?" she demanded. "Has the war begun?"

"Not around Megiddo," he told her. "We're in the eye of the hurricane for the moment, but you can feel the wind shifting."

"I don't understand," she stammered.

"It's like General Alizar said," Bronson explained. "The people of Israel have to fight. Everything in their history is being acted out in this time and in this place. Nothing makes sense to them except survival."

"I can't believe all this is happening and we're so far apart," Helen said with a tremor in her voice. "I want to hold you, Bronson. I feel like we're married to microphones when we should be . . ."

"Married to each other?" he asked. "Is that what you're thinking, Helen?"

"Yes," she admitted. "Yes, even though I know I'm going to lose you like I've lost everyone else who ever mattered to me."

"I love you," Bronson declared, "and I'm going to marry you when I get back. And I will get back. I promise."

Helen watched in horror as Bronson looked off in the distance, fear on his face. There was a deafening explosion, and the screen faded to black.

"Bronson!" screamed Helen.

"I'm okay," she heard him say over her earphones. "The explosion just knocked out the camera. We've still got voice."

"Are you all right?" she asked, choking back her own fear.

"It's happening, Helen," he told her. "It's getting worse. There's troop movement up ahead. One of the planes just dropped a bomb. I may have to change position." Helen heard another explosion. Then Bronson's voice crackling with static said, "That's it. I'm moving. I love you, Helen."

"And I love you, my darling," Helen whispered back. "God keep you safe."

Chapter 8

IT WAS EARLY AFTERNOON IN NEW YORK when Helen Hannah interrupted WNN's scheduled programming for an emergency report from the Middle East. An exhausted Bronson Pearl, his face shadowed by a two-day growth of beard, came onto the screen.

"We have now confirmed that Tel Aviv, Israel's largest city, has been struck by one or more chemical weapons," he reported through tight lips. "The exact nature of the poison is unknown, though it appears to be a fast-acting nerve gas absorbed through the pores of the skin. Thousands are believed dead already, and . . .

"A spokesman for the Israeli Defense Department is expected to make a statement at this time. We will be switching to the Knesset Building for that."

The scene switched to a somber man, standing at a podium, speaking angrily. ". . . an act both heinous and cowardly," he railed. "Poison is a weapon of genocide, a cloud of death meant to eradicate all human life."

He paused to compose himself then continued, "The

enemies of peace have accomplished nothing of military importance. Tel Aviv defense emplacements are unharmed. All communication links remain open. Airfields, missile emplacements, army barracks, weapon-storage units . . . all are untouched. This attack had only one purpose, to kill as many people as quickly as possible. We are estimating one hundred percent casualties among those who were outside when the bombs detonated."

"Are these the same terrorists who used gas in apartment buildings a few months ago?" asked the correspondent for the *Chicago Tribune*.

"Those cases remain unsolved so we cannot tell if the same people are involved," the spokesman answered. "We do not yet have samples of the substances found in those buildings for comparison. But they are quite similar in execution."

"Mr. Cohen," shouted a reporter for the *Los Angeles Times*. "Isn't your family living in Tel Aviv?"

"Yes," he said, his face suddenly tense. Several of the other reporters glared at the tactless reporter who had asked the question. Every reporter knew Ben Cohen's family was in Tel Aviv. They knew that only Cohen's job kept him from being by their side at this time. And they also knew that it would be a miracle if any of them were alive. "I have not heard from my family since the attack," Cohen continued, swallowing hard. "I do not know if they are alive. I do not know if anyone is alive. As many as two-thirds of the population of Tel Aviv may be dead right now. And my family may be among them." His speech was clipped, his jaw set, his eyes filled with tears. Several photographers moved in for close-ups, focusing on the type of poignant personal drama that sold the newspapers.

cلo

Dusk fell on Edna Williams's neighborhood, announcing the end of another day. Sadea Vadalia rolled down the steel shutters on the windows of her specialty shop. Herman Waring sat in a back booth of his diner reading a racing form. And James Misanno's Pizza Heaven gradually filled with the usual assortment of gang members, drug abusers, pimps and prostitutes, and latchkey teens. The café's outside walls were covered with graffiti: "R.I.P Little Tone"; "We loved you, Antoine"; "Kill the 83rd Street Rolling Gangstas." Several mom and pop "delicatessens" were open, but not to buy a corned beef sandwich or roast beef on rye. Instead the shelves were filled with cigarettes, forty-ounce bottles of malt liquor, condoms, and in the back room, cheap handguns. Cars moved slowly through the neighborhood with suburbanites cruising for action, drug dealers settling accounts, and lonely men looking for cheap motels that rented by the hour.

The neighborhood's elderly, like Edna Williams, sometimes felt as if they were living in a waiting room. Some would depart only in death. Some would leave for nursing homes. And most hoped that one day a son or daughter would move them to a spare bedroom in a safe suburb where they would finally be free of fear.

Yet where most saw despair, Edna Williams saw hope as she took to streets even most police avoided. "Folks aren't open to the Lord's message when everything in their lives is right," she explained to Pastor Holmes when he came to visit one day. "Look at those boys over there," she suggested, pointing out her apartment window at a half dozen gang members standing in the doorway of an abandoned building across the street. "See the tall one? That's Jo-Jo. His mother is a drug addict. The one with the cap is Angelo. His father used to beat him so badly, he has permanent nerve damage. LeMar's had so many different parents he doesn't know who to call Mom and Dad."

"You know these young men by name?" asked the astonished minister.

"Of course," she replied. "They're my neighbors. I've visited two of them in jail, but all of them have been in trouble with the law. They're all looking for love, structure, a family. They have a real spiritual hunger, Pastor. If we bring them the Word, they will turn their passions to the Lord. Their hearts are reaching out to Jesus; they just don't know it yet. That's what I tell them whenever I see them."

"And they listen?" queried the pastor.

"Of course not," she said with a smile. "They think I'm a crazy old lady. I know that in God's time their hearts will be reached by the Holy Spirit. Until then I just try to love them."

It was well after dark that evening when Edna returned to her apartment and turned on WNN. She sat in her favorite chair, to read from the Bible while keeping one ear open for her granddaughter on television. The image of Franco Macalousso appeared, surrounded by regional faction leaders.

Edna's Bible was open to II Thessalonians. Ignoring the reporter shouting questions to Macalousso, she read silently from the second chapter, "Now we beseech you, brethren, by the coming of our Lord Jesus Christ, and by our gathering together unto him, that ye be not soon shaken in mind, or be troubled, neither by spirit, nor by word, nor by letter as from us, as that the day of Christ is at hand." It was a familiar passage, one her Bible study had discussed a few weeks ago, and she wondered why it seemed so important to her now.

"Let no man deceive you by any means: for that day shall not come, except there come a falling away first, and that man of sin be revealed, the son of perdition . . ."

She glanced at the screen to see a close-up of Macalousso discussing the challenge of the new world order in this dire crisis. He spoke of negotiations, but the words faded away as she stared at him. There was something troubling about the man, a quality both greater and less than the image he presented. She glanced back at the Scriptures.

"And now ye know what withholdeth that he might be revealed in his time. For the mystery of iniquity doth already work: only he who now letteth will let, until he be taken out of the way. And then shall that Wicked be revealed, whom the Lord shall consume with the spirit of his mouth, and shall destroy with the brightness of his coming."

Edna set down the Bible. Something was happening, something she had instinctively known would occur in her lifetime, yet nothing she could ever have prepared for. She felt suddenly compelled to write a note to her granddaughter and hurriedly took up pen and paper. There seemed so little time, and so much to say.

∽

The terrified soldier ran up to Bronson Pearl, still broadcasting live from Megiddo. His face was pale, his stomach churning, and terror gripped his heart. As a Jew he understood that God's covenants with Abraham, Noah, Moses, and the other patriarchs promised that his people would survive. But such knowledge was of scant comfort now. He feared a lingering death, feared having to face God, knowing how many of his failings had been written in the Book of Life.

The soldier passed a printout to Bronson who, scanning it quickly, looked into the camera and waited for the signal that he was going live. "I have just been handed a report," he said, "that the U.S. aircraft carrier *Nebraska* has been struck by a tactical nuclear torpedo fired from a Chinese submarine. Ships in the area have launched search-and-rescue efforts, and helicopters have arrived, but the nine-thousand-ton ship was completely destroyed. The U.S. government is planning an immediate and retaliatory strike against key targets on mainland China, the Pentagon said in an official statement. We have unconfirmed reports that the president of the United States is aboard *Air Force One* and will make a declaration of war, which is expected to be endorsed by Congress."

As he spoke, the din of low-flying fighter jets drowned out his words. He cupped his hand around his earpiece to hear Helen's voice.

"Bronson, is there any word about how widespread the fighting is?" she asked.

"My understanding is that approximately three million troops were deployed within one hundred square miles of where I'm standing now," he replied. "Another two million men and women are reported to be less than three hours away, fully mobilized."

Several explosions shook the ground and the sound of automatic weapons erupted. Bronson reached for his gas mask, then signed off, "This is Bronson Pearl, WNN News, near Armageddon, Israel."

The picture went dark as Bronson and his crew raced for a shelter, managing to leap into protective trenches, dropping and rolling just as a hail of shrapnel struck the sand bags above their heads.

Chapter 9

THE BLACK BAG HAD ALWAYS BEEN a dark joke to the president. The Cold War, after all, was long over and the once mighty Soviet Union had crumbled. China was an emerging industrial giant, and its influence was overwhelmingly economic. Even trouble spots like Korea were geographically contained problems.

Only a few weeks earlier the chief executive and his Secret Service detail had even played catch with the little black bag. The notion that he had the special codes needed to trigger nuclear holocaust was simply beyond belief, even for a military man who had been trained to kill. But taking a life one-on-one was quite different from the horrors he now faced. Whole cities would be evaporated. The innocent would die with the guilty, and the living would curse their fate, envying the dead.

The survivors would be left with a land so poisoned that birth abnormalities, slow starvation and deaths by cancer would be inevitable. Victory would mean a bleak existence beyond comprehension, yet he knew he had to act.

The president took out his wallet to look at the snap-shots of his children. His daughter, Cara, lived in New York, a first-strike target for retaliation. His son Zachary was in Los Angeles, another first-strike target. Their youngest, Brad, was on a tour of England, a country that would soon disappear entirely from the map.

Doing his duty meant responsibility for the deaths of the children he loved, the grandchildren yet to be con-ceived. Tears streamed down his face as he ordered a courier to bring him the dreaded bag. It no longer mattered who was an enemy and who was a friend. The world was about to suffer unprecedented agony.

❧

Helen Hannah's dress was rumpled, her shoulders hunched, her hair disheveled, and her eyes red. It was the floor director who suggested she send out for something else to wear and perhaps touch up her appearance.

"World War III is breaking loose," Helen had snapped. "Who cares about seeing Suzy Sunshine? If the missiles launch, no one's going to care if I don't qualify for the Newscasters' Best Dressed List."

She paused as a voice from the control room announced that Dr. Stephen Horne was in the Los Angeles studio for a live interview. The UCLA professor was a lead-ing expert on nuclear research and development.

"Thank you for taking time to speak to us," said Helen as she returned to the set. A heavyset man with a round face and bushy white beard appeared on the monitor. "Dr. Horne," she continued, "we have heard that the Chinese used a tactical nuclear weapon against one of our ships on duty in the Mideast. Military experts are saying that a nuclear strike against one or more cities is a strong possibility. Just what exactly are we facing?"

"First, the obvious question is whether the president of the United States is willing to commit nuclear weapons," replied Dr. Horne. "A large number of missiles have already been removed from launch bunkers, but these can be retargeted quickly. At the same time, there are tactical nuclear weapons, some of which can fit inside a suitcase to be transported anywhere in the world without discovery. And certainly countries such as Iraq and Pakistan are likely to be able to launch a limited nuclear strike. The current international arsenal has an explosive force equal to four tons of TNT for every man, woman, and child on earth."

⁂

The president of the United States sat behind a small desk on *Air Force One*, facing the camera. Behind him was the Presidential Seal and he hoped the image would be reassuring.

". . . Approximately eleven minutes ago," he began, "we received confirmation that fifty-one ICBM's, each containing multiple nuclear warheads, had been launched against us and our allies. The attack on the U.S.S. *Nebraska* was intended to destroy our willingness to respond. That was a mistake. The loss of even three-quarters of our defensive emplacements would still enable us to destroy any enemy anywhere in the world. We are now faced with the most frightening event of human history. We are experiencing nuclear attack and must decide if we should retaliate. The answer, I am deeply saddened to say, is that we must, if we have any chance of surviving as a nation and as a people. Moments before this broadcast I ordered a retaliatory strike. I take this step with the knowledge that I am responsible to the people of America, and that to do less would be to deny our obligation as the leader of the free world."

❧

The WNN news set looked like a horror movie montage. One monitor carried live feed from the escalating battle in the Middle East. Another showed the firing of antiaircraft missiles from a coastal military position. A third replayed a tape of the president leaving the White House as a lead-in for his address from *Air Force One*. Various world leaders were also flashed on screens, some being evacuated, some addressing their citizens, and others meeting with Franco Macalousso. There were images of refugees fleeing advancing armies, abandoned children by the side of a road, crying mothers, and old people staring vacantly into the distance.

In one corner Helen and her staff focused solely on the monitor displaying a live broadcast coming from the Denver bureau. The reporter was standing at a major intersection in the city, close to where heads of the American government had taken refuge.

"For years Colorado has been headquarters for the Strategic Air Command," he remarked. "Many of the people in this city have worked for the military and grew up with the threat of nuclear war. Yet as the years passed, the fears lessened and the likelihood seemed increasingly remote—until today. Yet what is certain is that . . ."

Suddenly there was a deafening crash and the camera dropped to the ground, still broadcasting, showing cars run up against fire hydrants and telephone poles. There were screams in the distance, a sense of panic even from this skewed viewpoint.

Helen swiveled in her chair and picked up a headset. Holding the microphone near her mouth, she instructed the engineer to patch her through to the scene. There was no response. Looking up to the control booth, she saw a single person remaining; a young college intern. Although the room was soundproof, she could see his mouth contorted in a scream of pure terror.

Chapter 10

F AR BE IT FROM ME TO GOSSIP, Lilly, but I think that new girl in Cosmetics is . . . Well, you know." Ethel Bosley stood behind the checkout counter in Ladies' Blouses talking to her friend. The department store was quiet, the lunch hour crowd having dissipated, and the after-school rush of mothers and their children still an hour away.

"In a family way?" replied Lilly Nelson from Accessories, nodding. "She's put on five, ten pounds since she's been here, and you never see her eating much."

"And she's always mooning about that Proctor boy in Electronics," Ethel interjected. "They take their breaks together. They leave work together. They . . ."

". . . browse in Lingerie together," Lilly said, finishing her friend's sentence.

"Excuse me," said a customer who was trying to buy a blouse. "I hate to interrupt, but . . ."

The saleswomen glanced in her direction, then blithely continued their conversation. "I know for a fact that this girl is one of those six-month babies," said Ethel behind her hand.

"The apple never falls far from the tree," sniffed Lilly.

"Excuse me," persisted the customer. "I realize you're busy, but I'm wondering if . . ."

"Yes, we *are* busy," snapped Ethel.

Lord, give me patience, the customer thought and held up the blouse in her hands. "The blouse fits perfectly, but I'm afraid it's the wrong color. Do you have any others in back?"

"I suppose I could look," sighed Ethel, appraising the older woman with a critical eye. She didn't have time for someone making her run all over the stockroom before she made up her mind.

"It's to wear for a special event at my church," the customer started to explain.

"Yes, yes . . ." Ethel sighed dismissively, walking with deliberate slowness to the back of the store.

In the next moment, a scream caught her by surprise, a high, piercing wail of pure terror. She was sure the store was being robbed and turned, expecting to see one of the security guards rushing to the rescue. Instead she saw Lilly pointing to where the customer had been a moment before.

Ethel immediately assumed the woman had simply walked out, probably taking the blouse with her. Then she realized that a shoplifter wouldn't have evoked the fear she saw on Lilly's face.

"Gone . . . ," stammered Lilly, pointing. "She . . . vanished."

Ethel looked at the floor where Lilly was pointing. The blouse lay in a heap. But what was truly odd and unnerving were the old woman's clothes, neatly folded in a small pile with her glasses resting on top.

"She's gone, Ethel," Lilly said, her voice shaking. "One minute she was there. The next she was gone. Just . . . vanished . . ."

❧

Easton Blakely McNamara sat in the large motor home that served as his rolling office for the New Millennium Televival Ministry. The tent had been set up, the cameras were in position, and the satellite link was all set. Staff members were testing the two-way radios used for communication during the show.

McNamara had been on the road for more than a month now, and contributions were running 12 percent ahead of initial projections. And that was just the domestic gross. The language dubs for China, Italy, Germany, France, and several Eastern European nations were still being tallied and the financial returns from those countries would not be known for another three weeks. Only then could the bottom line—the impact of what was being called "the world's only television tent revival"—be fully assessed. If it all went as planned, Ellie Mae would have that Italian sports car she had been hinting about, and the kids could get the swimming pool they wanted for the Florida vacation home.

"The people from the Hinson Home are in their wheelchairs," reported an aide, who went on to assure the televangelist that the most elderly, rather frail-looking would be right up front during the broadcast. During the healing call, they would jump from their wheelchairs and rush down the aisles.

"Have you taken the information cards?" McNamara asked.

"Murray's running them through the computer right now," the aide reported. "When he gets the problems most often reported, he'll radio you as you work the crowd."

The so-called miracle healer checked the receiver he kept in his pocket, a thin wire running under his shirt and into a tiny earpiece. He removed the custom-made silk sports jacket he had purchased on his recent trip to London. It was inappropriate for the broadcast, and he kept a conservative polyester jacket bought off the rack from Sears to change into for work. He checked his hairpiece, removed his Rolex watch and his gold signet ring and, drinking the vodka-laced orange juice he needed before every performance, picked up his Bible and left the trailer.

The theme music was already playing as McNamara ran down the aisle, bounded onto the stage, and shouted his famed opening line: "Do you have the faith of a mustard seed?"

"Yes!" the audience shouted back, prompted by an aide who held up the audience cue cards. "Then let's move some mountains!" the preacher boomed, breaking into a rousing hymn in his rich, lustrous tenor that matched his rugged handsome good looks. Small wonder he was one of the highest-grossing preachers on television, a Christian recording star, and the head of a video distribution company that made millions from the tapes of his shows and the special productions available only through the ministry.

The show followed the tried-and-true formula the marketing staff had developed to gain the most response. The opening gospel number would be followed by Praise Time Testimony—taped interviews with people who claimed McNamara had changed their lives. But it was during the appeal for contributions that something went terribly wrong. Outside the tent, the sound of horns blaring and crashing cars startled McNamara, who glanced up at the engineer's booth, then looked away, dazzled by the spotlights. For a moment McNamara's vision was blurred. As it cleared, he was surprised to find himself surrounded by mostly empty wheelchairs. He spun around, realizing that most of the audience was gone, leaving only a few confused or frightened individuals, baffled staff members, and hired security guards. But the rest were gone and in their places, neatly folded and occasionally topped with eyeglasses, hearing aids, pacemakers, or crutches, were their empty clothes.

"Where is everybody?" asked McNamara in shock.

"Search me," said the voice of the engineer from the control room. "One minute they were there, then came that loud noise and suddenly they were gone."

McNamara tried to remain calm; there had to be a logical explanation. It was then he remembered what other ministers had tried to tell him in recent years—the ones who saw television as a means to bring God's Word to every corner of the earth, the ones whose fund-raising efforts were a vehicle for God's work, limiting their own salaries and spending the rest on teaching, missionary work, and other ministries.

For years he thought they were simply jealous of his success. His ratings were always higher than theirs, his weekly tally much greater. But now he realized they were sincere. They had given him books and videotapes and written long letters to him, trying to convince him that the events to come had been prophesied long ago. They had spoken of the Rapture, of a time of trial, of the reign of the Antichrist and the return of Jesus.

As he stared in wonder at the empty auditorium before him, McNamara wondered if they had been right after all, and that the Rapture had, indeed, come to pass. He would have to make a few telephone calls. He would have to find out how widespread this was and talk with other clergy. He would . . .

It was then he realized that the others might actually be gone, that he was alone among the televangelists who had remained behind . . . still not raptured, if that was truly what had just happened.

For the first time in his life, Easton McNamara stared into the cameras and didn't know what to say.

༺

The 18-wheeler barreled along a lonely highway in the Wyoming wilderness as the sun began to rise. It was going to be a perfect day for driving, Dan Mansfield told his passenger, Kevin. "What say come around six we pull off at some motel?" Dan added. "I'm too tired and achy to sleep in the cab another night. It's worth fifty bucks to get a good night's sleep." He looked over at the young man. "I'd be happy to share a room with you if you don't smell too bad and you don't snore. Besides, if I'm still awake enough, I think I'll go see if I can have a little fun."

"You're going to get a girl?" asked the hitchhiker. "I didn't think you were the type, what with all those pictures of the wife and kids you got in this rig . . . Or is that just for show?"

"I said fun," replied the driver. "Adultery's a lot of things, but fun isn't one of them. What I meant was that in these small towns there's usually one church or another's got a Bible study. Reading Scripture refreshes me more than just sitting in front of the tube. Want to come along?"

"Not my style," replied Kevin. "I got nothing against religion, but life's what you make it. You do good to people, they do good back. What goes around comes around. I don't need some preacher condemning me." He stared out the window at the rugged terrain and thought he'd be bored to tears if he stayed in a place like this for more than a week.

The rig began slowing and Kevin looked out the windshield. The road was straight with no accident or hazards in sight. The truck's speed continued dropping and he glanced at the radar detector, but it was silent. "Something wrong, Dan?" he asked, for the first time looking over to the driver, but Dan had disappeared, with only his clothing, neatly folded, left behind on the seat.

At that moment the rig began moving off the road. At the same time, a driverless car heading west crossed the median, spinning out in a gully while another driverless car slowed a hundred yards in front of them. Kevin grabbed the steering wheel and tried to move into the driver's seat before it was too late.

∾

They walked him to the small, sterile room wedged between the exercise yard and the prison infirmary. His hands were cuffed and a chain was wrapped around his body through the belt loops of his prison jumpsuit. He offered no resistance. Johnny Amsterdam had caused the warden no trouble in the last year and a half he had lived on death row. He had even been one of the intermediaries during the prison riot that, for a tense several hours, threatened to become a violent conflagration. But Johnny was a reluctant hero. He refused to see himself as special. More than a dozen years earlier he had murdered three people during a botched holdup and received the death sentence.

Then, for want of anything better to do, Johnny began assisting the prison chaplain, reading some of the books the chaplain brought, as well as tackling a study guide on the Bible. He had learned about Jesus, and His love for the lowest of society, and realized that Jesus had been a death row inmate just like himself. Johnny also knew that if he had lived in ancient time, his punishment would also have been the cross. He might have been placed next to Jesus, might have been the one to whom Jesus promised a room in His Father's house.

Johnny never talked of his change. The chaplain knew, and some of the guards, but Johnny felt that if the Lord wanted him to spread the Word, it could happen even on death row. And so he studied, prayed, and talked quietly to anyone who wanted to listen.

Behind a glass partition, in a viewing room several of the victims' family members had chosen to watch the execution and he took a moment to look into the eyes of each one, a look of deep sadness and regret. They wept as the cuffs were removed while he lay on a gurney. The chaplain recited the Twenty-third Psalm. Asked if he had anything to say, he only thanked the chaplain and the guards for their kindness. "This isn't easy for you, I know," he said quietly. "I understand that. The Lord God has brought us all to this place, just as He brought His Son to that hill so long ago. May we all know the peace of the Lord in Jesus' name."

The doctor administering the drugs attached an intravenous line. "I'm starting the Pentothol drip," said the doctor, quietly opening the valve and glancing at the IV bottle.

He was startled to see the line suddenly dangling, the liquid dripping onto the floor. The straps were in place, but they no longer encircled the prisoner's wrists and ankles. All that was on the gurney was the prison uniform of Johnny Amsterdam. The condemned killer had vanished.

༄

It was not a weapon, of that Judith Shimowitz was certain. Despite her grief over the loss of her family in Tel Aviv; despite the shock of the reports Bronson had been preparing; despite the nightmare of falling aircraft and out-of-control automobiles and trucks, this was not war.

As a college student in New York City, Judith had been an old science fiction movie buff, watching dozens of films from the 1950s, with scenes of death rays vaporizing people, and saucers coming down from the sky. She thought they were good for a laugh, naively simplistic and paranoid. But this was real.

One moment the people were there, the next all that remained were neatly piled clothing and personal effects. They had just disappeared.

She was frightened for the first time since the war began. She had lived too many years in Israel to be intimidated by war and terrorist bombings. She had grown cynical and pessimistic and believed in living for the moment. There had been times when she drank too much, said "yes" to things when "no" would have been the better answer. But actual fear . . . This was the first time. It was as though the world had gone out of control.

No. It was worse. It was as though the world was in someone else's control—someone evil.

Chapter 11

"THERE ISN'T ANY RIGHT ANSWER TO THIS," Bronson Pearl had told Bill Farkas the last time they had lunch together. It had been weeks earlier, before Bronson began shuttling between the Middle East and New York. "Those of us who make careers in broadcast journalism have a thirst for knowledge and we're paid to be nosy, but it's more than that. Even the worst, most biased newspeople, still seek the truth. It's just that some of them don't know it when they see it."

"I can relate to that," replied Bill. "But it's not the business. It's . . . Well, Lainie wants me to leave WNN. We've been trying to start a family, and though she hasn't said anything yet, I think she's pregnant."

"Do you want to leave broadcasting?" Bronson had asked.

"Not now," replied Bill. "Not when there are so many stories breaking and I'm getting a chance to be in the middle of them. It's all I ever wanted growing up. I'm not ready to make the change."

"Is your job worth your marriage?" Bronson probed. "What if Lainie wanted you to choose between the network and her?"

"She wouldn't do that," Bill insisted. "She's never had any illusions about the pressures of the industry. She knows she comes first."

Bronson sighed. "You have no idea how I envy your being able to go home to the woman you love each night." He reached out and touched his friend's arm. "If you're going to be a father, you need to be home."

Bill had agreed with Bronson. But he also knew he wasn't going to quit his job with the network. Lainie had wanted him to stay at home. "Call in sick," she urged. "Take a personal day."

"To do what?" he had asked, putting on his necktie.

"Take a walk in the park," she had pleaded. "Go to a coffee shop for lunch and just talk. Make love to me. I don't care what we do as long as we do it together."

"We can be together this weekend," he replied.

"If there is a weekend," Lainie had said ominously.

The remark had made him pause. "You're really scared about all this, aren't you, Lainie?" he had asked, not really wanting to hear her answer.

"Of course I am," she replied. "Neither one of us is thirty yet. We're just at the start of our adult lives. I don't want to miss the joy of growing old together."

He reached out to hug her. "We've been through this kind of brinkmanship before," he reminded her. "And nothing's ever happened. Millions were supposed to die from biological warfare during Desert Storm. The North Koreans were supposed to overrun the South and start a nuclear war."

Lainie had been adamant. "This is different. It's not a time for a husband and wife to be separated."

He had kissed her then, tender, lovingly. He loved her and she loved him. Nothing could ever change that.

Later that day Bill was scheduled to go live with man-on-the-street interviews when suddenly it was as if the world had gone mad. Cars swerved out of control, smashing into light poles, jumping curbs, breaking through department store windows. A police officer directing traffic suddenly vanished, only his uniform, shoes, and equipment belt piled neatly in the center of the street where he had been.

Two men washing windows on the thirty-second floor of a nearby building were startled when an attractive young secretary suddenly vanished from her desk. A bus traveling down Main Street turned a corner with approximately half the passengers it had previously been carrying, the driver striking an out-of-control car whose driver had disappeared.

Broken fire hydrants spewed geysers into the air and car alarms sounded their alert. Ambulance and police sirens began wailing in the distance and people in shock clutched at their chests with the onset of heart attacks.

Inside the nearby Bank and Trust, a robber demanding money fled in terror when the teller, the branch manager, and three of the customers suddenly disappeared. In the midst of the cacophony and mass confusion, Bill Farkas got a message from the studio to stand by for live broadcast.

∾

"Helen!" shouted the floor director moments after several WNN staffers had vanished. "Helen, where are you? What is going on around here?"

He was livid. One minute everyone was in place, lighting people, sound, camera operators . . . Then there was a sound and everyone was gone.

There was a scream and the director saw Helen Hannah on the floor by her desk. The scream had come from an intern who watched as a light pole one of the technicians had been setting into place had dropped when he disappeared, smashing the computer terminal, then striking Helen a glancing blow to the side of her head. "Somebody call 911," the intern shouted, grabbing some tissues to wipe the blood on Helen's face.

"Is she hurt?" asked the director, running over to help.

"Two minutes," he heard in his earpiece. It was the engineer's countdown to their return to the air.

"Throw in a commercial," he instructed.

"I'm okay," said Helen shakily. She kept her eyes tightly closed against the light.

"Stay still, Helen. The paramedics are coming," the director ordered.

"To do what?" she asked, raising her hand to touch the wound, and opening her eyes enough to see her fingers lightly spotted with blood. Wincing, she said, "I'm not going to die," and, trying to sit up, paused as a wave of nausea overwhelmed her. "But I'm not going to be able to go on air for a few minutes. I'll go to the lounge and lie down."

As Helen was helped from the studio, she glanced up at the catwalk where the lighting technician had been working when the pole dropped. It was then she realized that he was gone, and all that remained were his neatly piled clothes and his walkie-talkie.

A face appeared on a nearby monitor. "This is Ellie McPherson of WNN News substituting for Helen Hannah. While our bureaus in Washington, London, Moscow, and elsewhere try to get official statements, we will continue our broadcasts from the streets. Right now we're live with Bill Farkas, who has been talking with passersby in downtown Houston."

Farkas's face came into focus.

"Ellie, it's unlike anything I've ever seen," he reported. "It's not a bomb, or if it is, . . ." He was interrupted as a hysterical woman ran past, shouting the names of her missing children. The camera turned away from him and followed the woman. The woman fell to her knees, wailing, in front of three small piles of neatly folded clothing just below the window of a toy store. The television screen filled with her image, eyes wide yet sightless, overwhelmed by shock, clutching the clothing to her chest and moaning.

"This is unlike any weapon I've ever seen," resumed Farkas as the camera returned to him. "There was a sound like an explosion. At least I think there was. What I remember for certain was talking to people who then just disappeared, leaving piles of clothing where they had been standing a moment earlier."

"But is this some kind of death ray?" Ellie asked.

"I was hoping you could tell me," Farkas replied. "Nothing I know about would cause a human to simply vanish."

"It's happening all over the world, Bill," Ellie interjected. "Several have even disappeared here in the studio." In the back of the room, Helen had come back on the set and was anxiously asking, "Has anyone heard from Bronson?"

∽

Franco Macalousso stared out the window of the helicopter flying him to the Mount of Olives near the Western Wall in Jerusalem. It was there that he would at last ascend to his rightful place.

This is the land where the One who came before me walked and taught and healed the people, he thought. *Parlor tricks. He had no power. His time was then and they murdered Him. My time is now, and those who oppose me will be shamed when they see I am the bringer of peace. They will understand that true happiness will only come through living within my will.*

But he still felt oddly uneasy about the Rapture. It had to come, of course. He understood the Bible at least as well as the One who came before. The Rapture had been foretold, and what was foretold would be fulfilled. But what of those who were left behind?

Macalousso knew that all believers in the One who came before would be caught up to heaven. Otherwise he would have faced an army of believers, whose opposition would be unstoppable.

He also knew that those who rejected the One who came before, "who believed not the love of the truth," as the Bible stated, would be his most ardent supporters. It was they who would support his actions. It was they who would be his strongest allies. It was they who would be blinded by his powers as he brought peace to the world.

It was the others, those who had never heard the gospel before now, that worried him. He would need to keep such people from hearing the story of the One who came before. The homes of the raptured must be sealed and a search mounted to locate and destroy videotapes, books, and, of course, all Bibles. Detention camps had been prepared for those who might have heard the Word for the first time, football stadiums, ringed with razor wire and land mines.

"I have read the prophecies, too, President Macalousso," his assistant Len had told him. "And I know you are more powerful than any who can come against you. The Rapture eliminated your enemies."

But Len did not understand what the disappearances really meant. He did not understand that, while many would follow a new leader who could make them safe with his awesome power and seeming compassion, others might not. They might discover what they had not previously known. They might read what they had previously ignored.

But, he reassured himself, such thinking was counter-productive as he neared his moment of glory. His kingdom would soon be at hand and he basked in his triumph. It might take a while for some of those who were left behind to understand where the raptured had gone. By then he would have solidified his control and any opposition could be savagely suppressed by his new followers, the ones who had not believed the Word, who likened the life of the One who came before to mythology. "Franco Macalousso has brought a lasting peace," they would say. "We owe to him our total loyalty."

Macalousso inhaled and exhaled slowly, calming himself as the helicopter touched down. Overhead missiles were ready to strike their targets—an unimaginable military force was poised to unleash massive devastation. He could sense the worldwide panic of impending doom.

And he was pleased.

The first missile was seconds away from detonation when Macalousso stepped to the ground, faced the waiting cameras, raised his hands over his head, and shouted, "ENOUGH! WE WILL HAVE PEACE!"

His words were instantly broadcast throughout the world. Millions of television screens captured the image of Franco Macalousso, arms flung wide like a sorcerer unleashing his most powerful spell.

"ENOUGH!"

It was at that moment that air traffic controllers across the globe noticed several fast-moving blips disappearing from their screens. Pilots of long-range bombers radioed in to report that their bombs had disappeared from their holds. Their missiles had vanished and their controls no longer worked, except to guide them safely back to base.

The unthinkable horror about to be unleashed on the world was no longer possible. It was not that the hearts of world leaders had been changed. It was not old enemies who had become friends. But the threat was over. A new age had dawned, the age of Franco Macalousso.

Chapter 12

HELEN PACED THE PRODUCTION AREA like a caged animal. She had asked permission to fly to the Middle East, to join Bronson.

"There's no way, Helen," her producer insisted.

"But I'm talking ratings!" Helen retorted. It was a lie, of course. Overseas communications were down. Too many people had disappeared. The New York operation was barely holding together and Helen was one of the only anchors skilled enough to explain breaking stories to the viewers. But what she wanted was the assurance that Bronson was safe.

"You want to see if Bronson's all right because we're having so much trouble with our satellite link," the producer continued. "I'm sure he's okay. Now get back to work."

"Work?" Helen echoed angrily. She wanted to cry, to bury her head on the desk and sob. But she wasn't about to give her producer the satisfaction. "This isn't work. This is torture."

Fuming, she started to walk away, then realized suddenly that she hadn't been able to reach her grandmother since the crisis began. Returning to her desk, Helen tried to telephone the apartment. There were eight rings, nine, ten . . . still no answer, just Edna Williams's voice on her answering machine. She had called a half dozen times that day, and even tried the office of her grandmother's church, hoping someone would know where she was, but the church telephone also went unanswered.

She had to see Edna, had to make certain she was safe. Things were still too hectic at the network for her to go to her apartment. Tomorrow. She had been promised some time off tomorrow. She could stop on her way home.

∾

They gathered in the woods in Framingland, a small, rural Wyoming community too tiny for any map. The only business in town was a combination gas station, bar, restaurant, and general store and when anything more was needed, it usually fell to Joe Nelson to get it. He was the only one with an all-terrain vehicle large enough to hold a full supply of groceries from the "big city"—a town of 3,500 almost forty miles away.

Mostly people lived off the land, their only concession to modern life being solar panels to generate electricity or a hydraulic pump to bring up well water.

The true patriot protectors had begun to arrive within hours of the Rapture. Some reported seeing black helicopters hovering with high-intensity lights just before people around them disappeared. Others blamed the Mormon

Church, Jehovah's Witnesses, Avon Cosmetics, and Tupperware salespeople for what had taken place. What they could not decide was whether the disappeared were the enemy, part of a Communist military force, or were innocents being held prisoner. No ransom demands had been made, but a terrorist might be biding his time.

None of them had listened to President Macalousso's speech. They were convinced that the media were controlled by their enemies, though they could not be certain just who their enemies were so, instead, they gathered together in the woods far from prying eyes, deploying guards to protect the camp where they would build their paranoid new world.

❧

The work had been intense and she had eaten lunch at her desk, dozing over some computer printouts when she was awakened by the telephone. The shrill cry of the phone was so annoying and her groggy state of mind so numb that she almost missed what she had been waiting to hear. It was the news director, calling to tell her that a report from the Mount of Olives was coming in.

"Who's filing the report?" asked Helen, suddenly wide awake.

"Bronson Pearl," came the answer. "He's been asking about you, Helen. I told him you've been pretty much stuck here because of all the pressure."

"Bronson's all right?" she cried.

"Bronson's fine. We've had technical trouble out of the Middle East and this is the first time we've been able to re-establish our link."

She dropped the telephone and, running down the hall to the studio, took her position and attached the lapel microphone as she heard the countdown to going live.

"As you know we have had several hours without contact from the Middle East," she began. "However, we have restored communication and now have a direct linkup with Bronson Pearl, who is standing near the Western Wall in Old Jerusalem. Bronson?"

As Helen watched the monitor, Bronson Pearl appeared in the midst of a crowd of people gathered around the bright white stone of the Western Wall.

"Helen," he reported, "it's hard to know what to say about the events of the past few hours. No one alive today will ever forget where they were when they realized that imminent nuclear destruction was just moments away. Here, near the valley of Armageddon, it was then, as we have seen, that European Union President Franco Macalousso arrived to broker a comprehensive peace agreement. Yet, even as his helicopter was hovering, missiles were being fired from bunkers around the world. As President Macalousso stepped from his helicopter, the unforgettable, unexplainable event took place. Sirens wailed, cars crashed, planes fell from the sky as people simply disappeared off the face of the earth. Only their clothing and whatever else they were wearing at the time remained.

There was no smell of gunpowder, no burn marks from some sophisticated laser. They just . . . vanished. But in the midst of this incredible event, President Macalousso raised his arms and commanded it all to stop. He shouted to the winds, and suddenly there was peace. The missiles also vanished. They did not explode in mid-flight. They were not called back to the launch sites. They disappeared as though they never existed. A short time later, President Macalousso spoke to the nations of the world. We are replaying the speech he gave."

"Cut to the video," said the WNN engineer as Helen hoped there might be a break so she could speak directly to Bronson.

Footage appeared of the arrival of Macalousso's helicopter. "Citizens of the world," he began. "We are living in an extraordinary moment in history, a time when I have come to fulfill what is written. Until today I have been known for my work with the United Nations, and as president of the great union of Europe, a confederation larger than the Roman Empire, I worked among the leaders of the world to halt conflict, but I also refrained from bringing the real truth to the world until the appropriate time. Now you are at last seeing who I am, and the power I bring to lead you into your destiny. The people of the world will become one as we walk together toward the light of truth, a light hidden for more than two thousand years. You stood today on the brink of self-destruction, revealing the depths of your souls. You have shown your foolish pride and the hate that would lead you to the devastation of everything you have built, nurtured, and held dear. Parents were ready to kill their children, neighbors were ready to kill neighbors, leaders of nations were willing to subject their people to death in order to triumph over other people just like themselves. There were no restraints. There was no self-control. Your actions signaled that my time had come. I traveled to this spot, sacred for so many, to take my rightful place. I have spoken the word and the nuclear weapons have been vaporized. I have spoken the word and the chemical clouds have harmlessly dissipated. I have spoken the word and armed factions have set aside their weapons. And most important, because I understand your fears and worries, I have spoken the word and anyone whose mind was not open to the truth has vanished. Those who have disappeared were the hate-filled people with closed minds. Their continued presence would have prevented the evolution of those who remain. Like a weed removed from a garden, like a cancer excised from the body, you have been freed from their influence to grow into the beings I created you to be. Your destiny is beyond anything you ever imagined. My promise is that you will achieve that destiny. I have the power to do it! I have the power!"

Chapter 13

THE WALK TO HER GRANDMOTHER'S APARTMENT was
even more surreal for Helen Hannah. The near cataclysmic destruction that had been narrowly averted seemed
to have had no effect on the neighborhood.

A woman known locally as Crazy Connie was dancing
down the sidewalk while pushing a shopping cart piled
high with the clothing, eyeglasses, hearing aids, wallets, and
purses of the vanished.

A man who smelled of his own urine, with several teeth
missing and his face in need of a shave, lunged at Helen,
grasping her jacket sleeve with a filthy hand. He became dis-
tracted for a moment, letting go of her sleeve and wandering
toward another passerby, talking in a singsong voice.

The street people who lived in her grandmother's
neighborhood were handling the cataclysmic events the
best way they knew how. Some were nodding in doorways,
consuming anything intoxicating enough to blur the mem-
ory of the past few days. Others were babbling incoherently,
no longer able to grasp the difference between reality and

fantasy. Finally Helen arrived at the apartment entrance and rang the buzzer to her grandmother's flat. There was no response.

Helen reached in her purse and removed the keys her grandmother had entrusted to her. Climbing to her grandmother's floor she knocked, listened, then used the other key to get inside. As she entered the front hallway, her eye caught the flashing red message light on the answering machine. There were seventeen unchecked calls according to the counter display and she pressed the play button, listening to the first few messages.

"Edna? It's me, Doris. Have you been watching the news? It's just like Pastor Holmes was talking about last week. I really think this may be it. I think the day of the Lord could be . . . today."

"Grandma, are you there?" Helen heard her own voice. "It's me. Helen. Please call me as soon as you get this message."

"Grandma. It's Helen again. Please call me. I need to talk to you."

"Grandma, it's Helen. Are you all right? Grandma?"

"Grandma?" whispered Helen as she stopped the answering machine and started nervously down the hall. "Oh, God," she prayed, "let her be safe. Please let her be safe."

Helen heard a voice before realizing it was only the television. Her grandmother had left the set turned on. She moved to the kitchen where she found a half-prepared cup of tea, a pot on the stove, and a tea bag opened and resting on the side of the cup. On the floor in front of the stove were a dress, a pair of shoes, a hearing aid, and earrings, all in a neat pile. Helen also noticed the gold chain her grandmother wore and for the first time saw that attached to it was a key with a small piece of paper wrapped around it, and held in place with a rubber band.

Helen worked the rubber band from the key and opened the note. "My dear Helen," it read. "I will be gone when you read this, but do not worry. I'm with the Lord now. I told you about the Rapture and how I felt it would come in my lifetime. What I've been reading in the Bible is true, Helen, and though you have been left behind, it's not too late for you. God will help you and all those who ask. That is all you have to do. Just ask. The key is for a small box in which you will find some information you will need. Know that I love you even as we are apart. Grandma."

Helen stared at the note uncomprehendingly. This was not a suicide note. It was a message left by someone who knew she was going someplace—but where?

"Grandma . . . ," Helen whispered. She touched the clothing, tentatively at first, then lifted it to her face. She inhaled the familiar aroma of laundry soap mixed with a hint of perfume and closed her eyes, trying to imagine she was once again embracing the gentle Christian soul who had given her so much, comforted her so often, and loved her unconditionally. It was through her grandmother's self-less actions that she had first begun to understand the love of God, just as it was the loss of her parents that had some-how deepened her grandmother's own spirituality. And now she was gone, except for this note and this key. It was as though Edna was reaching out to her from . . . From where?

Helen took the clothing to the table, lovingly setting it down as though her grandmother might any moment come in and appreciate her folded blouse and skirt. She returned to the living room and, for an instant she was a little girl again, fearful she would be scolded for snooping in her grandmother's drawers, looking for secrets and treasures.

Tears filled her eyes. The finality of what was happen-ing was beginning to sink in, yet each time she touched one of her grandmother's belongings she expected her to return as if nothing had happened.

It was all so confusing, she thought as she began weep-ing again. She did not want to think about yet another loss, yet another loved one taken from her in an instant. She needed more time to talk, to ask the questions, get the answers she yearned for. She wanted to shout at her grand-mother for leaving her behind, an irrational impulse at once shameful and embarrassing. Yet she also knew it was all too human, part of a grieving process that might never be complete because she would never truly know where her grandmother had gone. But it was time to stop thinking so much. She returned to the search, looking for whatever might make some sense of the moment.

Meanwhile, the television in the living room continued to broadcast WNN reports from around the world.

The image of a tired General Alizar appeared. He had found himself on the front lines of the Israeli defense forces just seconds before the vanishing began. "I have never seen anything like it," said the somber general. He paused and looked away, dazed, as though living the experience all over again. "They were all over us," he continued at last. "As prepared as we were for their coming, their numbers were so vast there was nothing we could do. Our front lines were overrun and warplanes and missiles filled the sky. We knew that Jerusalem and Tel Aviv would be rubble within seconds, but there was nothing we could do but fight and pray. It all seemed so futile, so horrible. We knew what we would lose, knew that the bravest of our fighting men and women would die in the next few moments. It was then that we sent word to Bersheba, our nuclear site. We had made the decision that we were not going to go down alone. The prime minister had given the order to counterattack with every weapon in our arsenal." As the camera moved for a close-up, Alizar seemed to have aged ten years.

"Then it all stopped," he whispered. "I know no other way to describe what happened. I . . . I remember in my youth, reading in the Bible, of God's intervention in the lives of my people. But I thought they were just stories. Exaggerations. But only God Himself, directly intervening in all our lives, could have accomplished the miracle that has happened. Warplanes turned in their flight and returned to their bases. And the missiles were gone. Vanished. One moment they were in the sky, the next moment they were not. My eyes were not deceived. My mind was not clouded. They were there and they were not, all thanks be to God. And the ground troops, the thousands upon thousands of men who were advancing on my people, suddenly stopped as one. There was a silence, a serenity. It was as though a glorious peace descended. My fear had vanished. My anger was gone. I could embrace my enemy or my brother with the same joy." The general's voice became broken, tears filling his eyes. "Only later did we learn that the Messiah himself had returned to Jerusalem at that very moment."

ⁿⁿⁿ

Helen, looking through her grandmother's effects, heard the word *Messiah* and turned to the set to listen. A NATO officer was now speaking.

"I am not a religious man," he said. "I am not an emotional man. I deal with analysis, counter-intelligence, strategic planning . . . I know fact from fantasy. But I know what I saw. There were more missiles in the air than our people could keep track of. It was as though every one had decided to make a first strike, to win at all cost because there would be no second chance. None of us had ever conceived of such a possibility. Then silence came so suddenly I thought I had gone deaf. Everything just stopped. The missiles were gone. The radar could not track them. One minute it was a war to end all wars, to end all life. The next minute there was a peace such as the world has never known. I saw it all with my own eyes."

Helen moved to her grandmother's bedroom where a well-worn Bible was on the nightstand. A note attached to it read, "In the event of my disappearance, I want my grand-daughter, Helen Hannah, to have this Bible. The notes in the margins are my thoughts and prayers as I read it. The underlined passages will help her better know what has happened. I only wish I could be with her when she reads it, to show her how it can bring comfort."

Again Helen cried. She took the book, then continued looking until she found, on the floor of the closet, an old-fashioned strongbox. Helen used the key to open it, finding a videotape and some books inside.

⁖

WNN was meanwhile broadcasting from Jordan where the name General Assad flashed on the screen under the lean, hard, and weathered face of a man in his forties, a powerful figure and an obvious leader.

Behind him were tanks and troops preparing to leave the area and return home.

"We knew the Israeli defense forces," General Assad said. "We had studied them for many years, knew their strengths and weaknesses, knew the land. This was to be a textbook battle. We had planned our attack to overwhelm them, which we did. We thought the price would be worth the effort and we were on our way to victory. The trouble started with our radio communication. Everything was scrambled, and none of us could speak to each other. Our own language became impossible to understand. Then our tanks and trucks stopped, as though someone had taken the engines. Our mechanics checked the equipment and found it all to be working perfectly. Yet nothing would move. We tried to shoot our guns, to kill, yet bullets would not fire. Our handguns were useless, as well as our rifles. We did not think, in the midst of such panic, that Allah had returned. He had come to the Mount of Olives to make his message known. Allah delivered us from our enemies. Allah delivered our enemies from us. Praise be to Allah."

The broadcast switched to a Pentagon briefing room where Richard Stanfield was speaking. "I am speaking only for myself when I say I am not a religious man," he was saying. "Yet what has happened around the world must be the direct intervention of God. There can be no other explanation. A first-strike launch of three hundred missiles containing nuclear warheads would have eliminated an estimated two-thirds of the world's population. There was no power on earth that could stop what we had unleashed. No one was protected. We had launched forces from all sides that should have ended life as we know it. But the fact that I am here today proves that the hand of God is in the affairs of men. It is God who let me live. It is God in whom I believe with a faith that cannot be shaken."

Helen turned off the television and slipped the tape her grandmother had left into the VCR. A program entitled "Left Behind" appeared on the screen. In it Jack and Rexella Van Impe were talking about the Rapture, Armageddon,

and the last days. The tape had been cued to a specific segment of the program that she realized her grandmother
probably wanted her to watch.

"Well, Jack, we've talked about all these signs of the
times," Rexella was saying. "But what is the next thing that
the Bible says we should be looking for on the prophetic
calendar?"

"Rexella, what we're watching for now is something
called the Rapture of the Church," replied Jack. "Any day
now, every one of us who has accepted Jesus as our Lord
and Savior is going to vanish off the face of the earth. It'll
happen according to the Bible, in a moment, in the twin-
kling of an eye. First Corinthians 15:52."

Helen listened, intrigued, as they talked. She opened
the Bible she had found in her grandmother's bedroom,
looking for the passages they were describing. As she listened and read, she felt both amazement and encourage-
ment. It was as though her grandmother's final words were
being taught to her anew.

"Oh, Jack, it is so exciting," said Rexella on the tape.
"It's something every Christian is so looking forward to. But
what about those who are left behind? We all have friends
and loved ones who aren't going to know what's happened.
So what will become of them after we all vanish?"

"Well, Rexella," replied Jack, "the Bible tells us that
after the Rapture a great world leader is going to arise on the
scene and he's going to try to explain the whole thing away.
Not only that, but he's going to take credit for saving the

world from destruction. In fact, he's going to try to make those left behind believe that he is actually the Messiah, but the truth is that he's nothing but an impostor empowered by Satan himself."

Helen wanted to deny what she was hearing yet knew the words being spoken were true. She continued reading the passages the Van Impes were quoting, focusing, fascinated, on every word.

The last segment of the tape featured evangelist Luis Palau. As tears rolled down her cheeks, she listened as he spoke. "So the answer to all of this is simple. Just ask God to come into your hearts. For those of us now, living before the Rapture, we can join our Lord in heaven before the Antichrist even comes to power. But even after the Rapture, the love of God and His mercy are still available. But you've got to take the first step. You've got to get down on your knees and ask God to come into your life. Admit you are a sinner and open your heart to Jesus. If you do that simple thing, that simple act of faith, you will have eternal life."

It was dark outside when Helen, still sobbing, dropped to her knees and began to pray. Finally she understood. Finally she understood what her grandmother had carried in her heart all those years.

"Dear God," Helen prayed. "Please forgive me for being so stubborn. Somehow I always knew Grandma was right when she told me that I needed You to wash away my sins. I read about Your Son. I spoke of Him with my lips. But now I know that was not enough. Lord, I ask You now, please come into my heart and into my life. Forgive my sins." And as she prayed, she felt the enveloping warmth surround her. And she realized that the God whom she denied had always been with her. It was she who had refused to open her eyes, her mind, her heart to what was always there for her. Her grandmother had been but one of many vessels for His love. And while she missed Edna and always would, she at last understood that it was God who would hold her, nurture her, love her unconditionally, if she would only reach out and embrace Him.

". . . in Jesus' name," she whispered, "amen."

Chapter 14

THEY GATHERED TOGETHER in wonder and joy, sharing miracles of the past few days. They had heard about the Messiah, of course, and many of them called themselves Christians, but their faith had long since lost its meaning.

Franco Macalousso was their savior now, a man who made missiles disappear in mid-flight, whose deeds were recorded on videotape and shown on the evening news. This was truly the Messiah, not a myth written long ago. He was the one to whom they gave praise and honor, the one who made them feel blessed to be alive in such a time of peace, harmony, and hope.

The headlines said it all: "Macalousso Saves the World." "Public Has No Doubt: Macalousso Is the Messiah." "Heaven Applauds the New Messiah."

But there was a handful of other people who had begun reading the books and watching the videotapes left behind by the vanished ones. Like Edna Williams, a few had deliberately left material for relatives or friends, material carefully placed on shelves or on tables to be found by a well-meaning landlord, neighbor, or police officer. The information this handful of people discovered was so amazing that some had tried to share it with coworkers and relatives. It was then they discovered that the full prophecy of the Rapture had indeed been fulfilled. Those who accepted Franco Macalousso as the Messiah could no longer hear the truth. They found growing hostility within their families and friends; fathers against sons, mothers against daughters, husbands against wives, so they gathered in two's and three's in Jesus' name, meeting in coffee shops and living rooms, and those few churches Macalousso had let stand.

The names on the List were another matter. This List, a registry established by Len Parker using the internationally linked computer repositories of law enforcement agencies, identified the "fanatics" who had embraced Christianity since the coming of the new Messiah. Their names and locations were kept on file for future reeducation if possible, and if not, at the very least, containment to keep them from spreading their poison. The List was also a means for the quiet confiscation of the material left behind by the raptured, books and videos that were of no value now that the new Messiah was here to reinterpret past and present. "Did the One who came before stop wars?" he asked. "Did the One who came before bring peace? Did the One who came before take missiles from the sky? Only a Messiah can do what I have done. Only a Messiah could change hearts filled with such hate. I am the one foretold, the one who has brought true and lasting peace. And now that my time has come, there must be no other."

Yet those who gathered secretly in two's and three's knew better. They believed in He who Macalousso was calling the "One who came before" and knew Him as the true Messiah. The boldest among them declared the truth to the world, phoning into talk shows to bring the truth to the listening audience, explaining passages in the Bible that foretold this time, encouraging others to study the Word and think for themselves.

Others researched the lives of the raptured, discovering how loving they had been, how Spirit-filled and Spirit-led good works had come naturally to them. For the most part, they were met with pity, anger, and hostility.

Many new Christians, now called the "Haters," were berated for their lack of belief in the true Messiah. They were attacked, beaten, and shot. Firebombs were hurled at their homes and hate messages were scrawled on doors. Tolerance for the old beliefs was running low and patience for the enemies of Macalousso wearing thin.

⁂

Bronson Pearl had not told Helen of his return home after his assignment in the Middle East. He had slept on the plane coming to America, shaved, brushed his teeth, made himself as presentable as possible before seeing her again. He wondered if she understood the significance of the last few days. Had she seen how fleeting life could be? One minute she was in his arms, and the next he was standing at Armageddon, broadcasting the end of the world back to her anchor desk in New York. They should have been together then. They should be together now.

Helen was in a staff meeting when Bronson walked into WNN, transfixing her with his presence. Seeing him in the flesh, knowing she could rush across the room to embrace him . . . Helen smiled, tears coming to her eyes. Then she mouthed the word "Yes."

Bronson looked at her quizzically, shrugging his shoulders.

"Yes," she said aloud, rising from her chair and hurrying over to Bronson. Oblivious to the crew, she put her arms around him. "Yes," she said. "Yes, I'll marry you."

∽

They had moved quietly into WNN headquarters. Young men chosen especially for their loyalty to Franco Macalousso. Their uniforms identified them as carrying his authority, transcending all others.

Bronson had seen this type of soldier before. Macalousso had prepared such a force while still with the United Nations and they were with him as European Union security. Now that he had revealed himself to be the Messiah, they were to play an even more prominent role.

It was a thought that troubled him. If Franco Macalousso truly was the Messiah, why did he need so much security? He had halted global destruction, somehow removing the missiles from the skies. Those who believed would follow without question. Those who opposed would dare not challenge him.

So why these armed men in key communication centers? It was a question he felt almost guilty asking, considering what he had witnessed with his own eyes. After all, he had returned safe and sound to the woman he loved. The woman who sustained him when all about them was insanity.

"It's good to be back, Helen," he told her later that day as they coanchored the evening news. "Actually, it's good to be anywhere."

"You're right about that, Bronson," she replied, smiling. "For those who just tuned in, we're expecting President Macalousso to address a worldwide audience from Jerusalem. He has promised to shed some light on the incredible events of the last forty-eight hours. From the numbers we've received, this will be the most-watched telecast in history." She looked up at the control booth and nodded. "We've just been told the feed is ready." She turned to the camera. "We now switch live to Jerusalem."

The rally was being held in a stadium with spotlights positioned to regularly sweep a crowd estimated to be over seventy-five thousand, with another one hundred thousand outside watching the speech on giant television monitors.

Helicopters hovered overhead from a dozen television networks around the world. Reporters roamed the crowd, reporting to outdoor venues that had been established in other parts of the world so the speech could be witnessed live by communities of every size. At least two billion people were expected to be listening, either in public gatherings or on home televisions and radios.

Franco Macalousso walked calmly down a long aisle. A spotlight focused on his figure as he made his way to the podium. On catwalks overhead, snipers had been positioned; reporters who had questioned the need for such security were told not to mention it on the air or to discuss other security measures taken for the event. As a result, the televised image showed Macalousso walking unprotected and unconcerned as the huge audience rose to its feet, cheering.

"Franco! Franco! Franco!" came a massive cry from the crowd. "Praise the holy one! Franco! Franco! Franco!"

Unknown to the mass audience, protests in some of the broadcast areas were also under way. A group calling itself "The Friends of Jesus" had come together, their clothing stitched with biblical references to the Antichrist. They were ignored, then taunted, and finally spat upon by enraged crowds. But the ardent converts continued to spread the Word, gathering in New Delhi, Manila, Mexico City, Vancouver, and elsewhere. There were numerous arrests, with local police taking the side of the angry mobs. But in Jerusalem, the broadcast continued without interruption.

The cameras focused on an object Macalousso carried on his walk to the podium. It was a large, leather-bound Bible, obviously much used. As he reached the dais, he raised the book high in his right hand.

"Ladies and gentlemen," he declared. "I hold in my

hand what can only be considered the most misunderstood book in the history of the world. It is in this book that my coming has been foretold. It is in this book that you have also read of the Great Deceiver, the One who came before. The prophet Zechariah spoke of my coming today. He foretold, 'And his feet shall stand in that day upon the Mount of Olives, which is before Jerusalem on the east.' A long time ago, the One who came before spoke in my name and deceived many. His deception continued for almost two thousand years, but now I have removed those who believed His lies, those who chose hatred and intolerance over peace and unity."

He paused, gauging the audience reaction. As his amplified voice boomed across the stadium their adulation grew louder, cheering the words even as he spoke them.

"I have removed the tares from the wheat," Macalousso declared.

Some had tears in their eyes, others had their heads bowed, their eyes tightly closed in prayer, with open hands raised toward the sky. "Thank you, Franco," they sobbed. "Oh, Franco, thank you."

But there were also angry cries, though the television audience never heard them. Roving security forces would grab the protesters and force them to their knees, with the pretense of searching for weapons, as they were escorted away. Watching in the WNN studio, Helen felt her own anger rise. "Bronson, it's a lie," she declared. "I read what Grandma left for me."

"Shhhh," said Bronson. "I want to hear this. I met the man, spent hours with him. He's fascinating."

"He's a vehicle for Satan's lies," she insisted.

"Helen, just watch," Bronson insisted. "Please. I want to hear what he has to say."

"I have come in peace," Macalousso was declaring, "and I have brought peace to the world."

"Franco! Franco! Franco!" the crowd chanted.

"I have saved you all from destruction!"

"Praise his precious name. Franco! Franco!"

Gesturing to the Bible, he continued, "This book has told you that by my fruits you would know me. Now that you have seen the works that I have done, know that your salvation is at hand!"

Chapter 15

HELEN GLANCED AROUND THE NEWSROOM where everyone was riveted to the monitor. Even Bronson was staring, though Helen could not read the bemused expression on his face. "This reminds me of Hitler in the 1930s," he whispered to her. "Did you ever see those clips? This guy's got the same gift of oratory. Fascinating." She felt a tightness in her chest as he added, "Thank God this one's for real. Hitler was a dangerous fraud. I've seen the power of this man with my own eyes."

"I am here to tell you today that mankind is ready to take its next great step of evolution," Macalousso continued. "I will show you the wonderful powers that lie within you waiting to be unleashed, powers that have been your birthright from the beginning. Those who were not ready, those whose minds were closed to the truth, have been removed. Only the fittest have survived, and that is why you are here with me today." The cheers were deafening as he shouted over the tumult, "Those who refused to believe in the power of the human mind have held you back. They believed that our true power came from outside of ourselves. I tell you today, the power is within you. It always has been. And now, it is time for you to see what you are capable of. I will be your guide. The power is within you!"

Despite her new understanding, Helen suddenly realized that she, too, was riveted to the television monitor. There was something more than charisma that gave power to President Macalousso's words; a force within him was so seductive it could overwhelm the very soul of the unsuspecting. She glanced at Bronson Pearl and realized from his face that he was no longer dispassionate, but like the rest of the world he was mesmerized by the image on the screen. She needed to break the spell, needed to speak with Bronson alone. Reaching across the desk, Helen took a pen and paper and wrote, "I need you to leave here with me right NOW!"

Bronson looked at the note, puzzled. This was the most important speech by the most important person in human history. Watching a tape or reading a transcript later just wouldn't be the same.

He looked at Helen and shook his head, pointing to the monitors as if to say, "Wait. Not now."

Helen took the paper and angrily wrote, "PLEASE!!"

Bronson looked at her more closely. Helen was an experienced professional and if she was this insistent, it must be something more important. He rose to his feet and quietly started across the room. Helen left a few moments later.

Overhead in the control room, Len Parker was the only

person not watching Macalousso. Quietly, he tapped the shoulder of a uniformed soldier at a control desk. "Rewind surveillance camera three, then run it on monitor six," whispered Parker, pointing to a screen only he and the soldier could see.

As the tape ran Parker watched until Helen's paper was passed to Bronson the first time. "Stop! Now give me a close-up on that," he commanded.

The words on the note filled the screen.

❧

Helen reached the side entrance of the studio, opened the door, and walked outside.

She met Bronson in a place they both knew was safe from the prying eyes and ears of Macalousso's squads. There were no windows on this side of the building; they had gone there before when they sought privacy. Helen embraced Bronson, clinging to him fiercely, her body shaking from the release of tension. Finally she stepped back, her hands on his shoulders, her head bowed. She breathed deeply, exhaling slowly. "Lord, give me the strength . . . ," she whispered.

"What's this all about, Helen?" he asked. "I don't think I've ever seen you this upset."

As Helen started to speak, she noticed in the distance two men, one in a suit and the other in a uniform. She took Bronson's arm and hurried with him around the building to where she had parked her car. "Just get in," she said urgently. "We're being followed."

Helen drove onto the freeway, getting off at the first exit then getting on again, to shake their pursuers. She returned finally to the city, heading to a parking garage near her grandmother's apartment, and, satisfied she had lost the surveillance team, headed to her grandmother's apartment building.

"I know this is about President Macalousso, Helen," Bronson said when they were safely inside. "I know you saw it on television, but you really had to be there in the midst of it. The missiles were launched, the battle was inevitable, and suddenly a helicopter landed at the Mount of Olives. Just as the door opened and Macalousso stepped to the ground, the weapons vanished as though they were playing cards in a magician's hand."

He paused, realizing that Helen did not share his enthusiasm. "No impostor or charlatan could pull that off," he insisted. "This guy is beyond anything we've ever seen. If he's not who he says he is . . . then who is he?"

"I'd rather you saw it for yourself, Bronson," she replied. "Grandma knew I wouldn't understand before she was raptured, so she left something to help me. Now it's your turn. Watch the tape and we'll talk. But I have a feeling your questions will have been answered."

Helen inserted the tape, and turned on the television. Rexella and Jack Van Impe appeared on the screen.

"So, Jack," Rexella was saying, "millions of people will suddenly vanish off the face of the earth. The world will be in peril as never before and then suddenly a great leader, unlike anyone the world has ever seen, will rise and seem to bring total peace to mankind."

"The Bible spells it out in perfect detail," replied Jack Van Impe. "He's going to quarterback a seven-year peace treaty, as Daniel 9:27 shows us. Then he's going to seemingly bring peace to the whole world as I Thessalonians 5:3 reveals. He is going to be the most compelling political leader history has ever seen. But he's much more than that. He's nothing less than a great deceiver, as II John verse 7 shows. He's the one the Bible calls the Antichrist in I John 2:18. And he has only one goal, to deceive the world into believing . . ."

Bronson stared at the set as the tape finished. "It's fascinating, all right," he said at last. "How many of those people are still around?"

"Bronson," replied the exasperated Helen. "Don't you see that this is about what we're experiencing right now? Don't you see that Macalousso is going to tighten his hold on communications to hide the truth? Do you think the Antichrist is going to let us reveal his secret to the whole world? We can't let that happen, Bronson. We've got to tell . . ."

"Helen, back up a bit," he interjected. "I know you're grieving the loss of your grandmother. And I grant you this stuff is interesting. It does provide a reason for what's happened, but so does Macalousso, and I don't see where one version is better than the other. Certainly an old cynic like you isn't going to take all this literally."

Helen glared at him. "My grandmother is not dead, at least not as we normally think of death. How many of the raptured are there? Millions, at least. But there has been not one report of a corpse, or a mass burial ground. Bronson, I miss that woman. You met her. You knew her. The truth is that she was either raptured or Macalousso is telling the truth. And that would make my grandmother a follower of something false, a menace to society. Franco Macalousso's no hero. He's the Antichrist and we need to expose him."

"For God's sake, Helen you're a journalist," retorted Bronson. "We're witnesses to the greatest event in the history of the planet and you're talking to me about the bogey-man."

"What does it take to convince you, Bronson?" asked the exasperated Helen. "Can't you see it? You've heard Macalousso. You've heard what he said about the vanished people. Either he's telling the truth or he's the Antichrist. It's all right here in the Bible. You've got to see that."

"I'll tell you what I see, Helen," Bronson replied. "I see someone who needs to step back for just a minute. We all want answers. But you and I can't let that desire cloud our journalistic judgment. It's time for a reality check. We've been through a lot, but we're still doing our jobs because that's how we keep our sanity. This thing with your grandmother . . . Helen, I'm sorry. I loved the woman too. I don't know why she's gone, but you've got to get a grip on yourself so we can go back to the studio and . . ."

"I'm not going back," said Helen firmly.

"What are you talking about?" demanded Bronson.

"I'm not going back," she repeated. "If you're still blind to what's going on . . . well, that's between you and God.

But I know the truth about Macalousso. I know the truth about my grandmother."

Bronson sighed. "Of all the people I know, I would have thought you'd be the last to get caught up in some . . . religious cult."

"What you can't seem to understand, Bronson Pearl, is that I am using every bit of objectivity that I've learned as a journalist," Helen insisted. "I'm emotional about Grandma. I'm emotional about almost losing you. But I am coldly objective about what is taking place right now. You're the one with the steel-trap mind that closed before reality could set in. This is for real, Bronson Pearl. What's it going to take for you to believe that?"

"Look, Helen," he countered, "you've got to agree that for both of us, seeing is believing. But I'm not certain you're still doing that. I think you've got a belief system and want to see only what supports it."

"Maybe it's you who is refusing to see what doesn't support your beliefs," Helen shot back. "Maybe you're not ready to fall on your knees and give your heart to God, to embrace the teachings of His Son, and frankly I'm not asking you to do that. All I'm asking you to do is to look at this objectively. Don't just think about the missiles disappearing from the sky. Think about the security forces that are quietly moving into our lives. Think about the life my grandmother lived. Think about me and the fact that if I didn't really believe all this, I wouldn't be asking you to take it seriously." Helen paused, emotionally drained, her voice filled with disappointment. "Of all the people I know, I'd have thought you'd be the last to dismiss something without even looking into it."

"I'm not saying there's nothing to it," Bronson replied bitterly. "My own father spent his life believing it and it made him a happier man. Maybe it even made him a better man. But he still ended up dead, just like all of us will."

"His earthly body may have died, Bronson," Helen told him, "but his soul is still very much alive."

Bronson stared at Helen for a moment, then he took her hand and brought it to his face, holding it against him, feeling her warm touch. "I wish I could believe that, Helen, honestly I do."

This was a difficult time for them both, but Helen realized that as deep as their differences were, she still loved him. He rose to walk around the room, talking as much to sort out his thoughts as to try to convince her of anything.

"Look, I've met President Macalousso," he said. "I've seen what he's done with my own eyes. I followed his career at the United Nations. I interviewed him when he became president of the European Union. And I was there in Israel, there in Armageddon." Bronson paused, realizing the impact of the word he had just used. "Franco Macalousso is the farthest thing from evil that I have ever seen. Think about what he's done. He rid the world of hatred."

"Except for those people who disagree with him, who love Jesus, embracing Him as their Lord and Savior," replied Helen.

"He saved us all from destruction," was Bronson's retort. "And now all he wants to do is unite the world in peace. I know you want me to look at the Bible. Helen, I've looked at it. Yes, I have an interest in religion too. But I'm still a journalist. We get Jesus filtered through the ages. But I was there for the arrival of Macalousso. I saw him raise his arms and make missiles vanish from the skies, weapons cease functioning, and millions of men and women stop in the midst of battle. I saw him, Helen, I was a witness. This man is who he says he is, Helen."

Helen sighed. "Maybe it's time for you to step back and look at this as an objective journalist. He's done some fantastic things and he's making even more fantastic claims about himself. He's impressive, unlike anyone we've ever encountered in history. But there's also evidence to show that he just might be an impostor. Let me get some paper, a Bible, and a few of my grandmother's reference books. We can sit down and start checking this out."

Bronson started to object, then realized that, at the very least, they would be stronger for working together. "Okay," he said. "Let's take it from the real beginning. The Bible says this Antichrist character will come out of the Roman Empire, right?"

❧

They sat in the car, watching and listening, through the tiny transmitter in the overhead light fixture in Edna Williams's kitchen, similar to hundreds of other such devices placed in the homes of those who had disappeared. Helen Hannah had been monitored on each of her visits to her grandmother's home. Now that she had brought Bronson Pearl there, a minor complication had arisen, but no individual was as important as the Messiah and, as trusted as Bronson might be, he was also expendable.

The image on the monitor was fuzzy, but their faces were identifiable and their voices were coming through clearly.

An agent checked the recording meter as Helen was heard saying, "That's right. The Antichrist will come from the Roman Empire, and according to this encyclopedia, the European Union is geographically equal to what was known as the Roman Empire of biblical times."

The agent smiled and said to his partner, "The sound's perfect. All we have to do is sit back and let them incriminate themselves."

✥

It was midnight before Bronson started to see that what Helen was saying was based on more than emotion. They had gone through two pots of coffee, and both were exhausted, but neither was ready to stop. They had another Van Impe video playing on the TV, and all around them were books. Bronson was using a Bible, scanning each page until he found the passages he wanted. In front of him was a piece of paper divided into two columns. On the left was a column marked "Prophecy." On the right was a column marked "Fulfilled."

The Rapture headed each category. There was no question that it had happened, no question that it had been foretold. Bronson admitted as much to Helen. She was right. Edna Williams did not fit the Macalousso profile of the vanished population. The truth had to be 180 degrees from what he claimed. Then there were the heart attacks. The incidents had begun right after the Rapture. At first the victims seemed to be only the elderly and frail, experiencing the shock of seeing friends and loved ones suddenly vanish. But they realized that such deaths were statistically abnormal, even for a natural disaster such as a flood or hurricane. The sheer number of heart attack deaths had to be the fulfillment of prophecy. Nothing else made sense.

The notes Bronson made each represented a prophetic promise, and each had been fulfilled, except for the foretelling of a peace treaty between Israel and the rest of the world. But such a treaty, with a seven-year duration, was the only prediction yet to be realized.

Bronson put down the Bible, picked up the paper and studied it. He looked from the left column to the right, left to right, again and again. The conclusion was inescapable, but he did not want to deal with what he was seeing. Finally he stood up and began pacing the room.

"I'm sorry, Helen," he said. "I just can't accept this. I understand where you're coming from. This stuff is interesting. No, it's downright compelling. I don't know how to say this; I'm a journalist, a professional reporter. I'm supposed to be the most trusted man in America." He smiled.

"I even have my own theme music. But I can't believe we should be worrying about the bad dreams of some ancient shepherd," he said with a sigh. "Look, Helen, I'm heading back to the studio. I'll cover for you as best as I can until you have some time to think about this. I can't buy into your fantasy no matter how much I love you."

He crossed to the door, then paused, looked back to her, and said, "You tell your God that if He is real, and if He has something to say to me, He knows where I live. Maybe you have to be touched in some special way, and if that's what has to happen to me, so be it. For now, with all that I've seen over the last few days, I can only say that a God in the real world is worth two in any book."

Chapter 16

T HERE WAS INTENSE MEDIA PRESSURE concerning the actions of those now called the Haters, the ones who insisted on following the Man whom Macalousso called the One who came before. A number of tabloid-style television personalities began to take advantage of the suddenly available time blocks vacated by Christian broadcasting. Kenny Casswell, the host of the widely syndicated "Kenny C's People," was the most popular.

"I can't speak for the good Lord above," said Kenny Casswell during the opening commentary on his new show. "God is the ultimate judge, and what He says goes. I just know that a lot of sinful, hateful, hypocrites have been removed to make way for the coming of the Messiah. I just wish my ex-wife could have been one the Messiah removed! And now, before I bring out Angel McMillan, who sings the praises of Macalousso as sweetly as her name implies, I want to say, thank you, glorious Messiah. Thank you for this chance for me to glorify you in prime time. And thank you for Angel McMillan, whose album of your favorite songs will soon be released. It is called *Music For The Messiah* and is available in record stores everywhere."

Casswell's top-rated show was followed by local newscasts featuring stories of church defacements, which were in their "happy news" segments, as were attacks against those rare individuals who dared speak the name of Jesus. They were seen as an evil force, subversive, and evil.

Franco Macalousso's frequent speeches spoke of tolerance, love, and harmony, but he also made clear that anyone who stood against such values was an enemy and must be stopped. Uniforms had been distributed to the Women Who Watch and other loyal groups supplementing local police and military to isolate the Haters, who were kept in hospitals, minimum security prisons, and specially created camps until they could see the error of their ways. To Macalousso followers, the enforcers were heroes of the new world order. To the Christian underground they were simply "Macalousso's Marauders." The Marauders spray-painted "Death to the Haters" and other slogans on the doors and walls of churches and storefront meeting halls, defacing the homes of people suspected of being active Christians.

Some looked upon the Jesus believers with pity, knowing that in the near future they would face the wrath of the Messiah. Already there were arrests, jailings, and sentences that ranged from forced reeducation to life in prison. But others were filled with loathing, smashing windows, firebombing homes and apartments. Beatings were increasingly common and in one community, a group of zealots calling themselves the "Army of Macalousso Consciousness," surrounded a cluster of homes where Christianity had blossomed from a time shortly after the Rapture. The residents, herded onto a school playground at gunpoint, called themselves the "Descendants of Peter," referring to the biblical passage that described Peter needing the Resurrection to become a full believer. They had not known Jesus before the Rapture, but now formed a resistance movement based on their own conclusions. After the Rapture, with writings and tapes to guide them, they knew firsthand the unerring truth of Bible prophecy, transforming them from religiously ignorant men and women to people totally committed to their faith. Some were shot for their proselytizing, and died rejoicing in their martyrdom, refusing to renounce the Lord.

&

Bronson Pearl, for one, was troubled by the growing violence. On the surface the world was at peace. Old enmities had fallen away. People no longer lived in fear. Yet the antagonism toward the new Christians was growing. Even if they were following a false prophet, believing Jesus as the true Son of the living God, they still prayed for those who professed allegiance to the new Messiah. They threatened no one with their unconditional love.

Equally troubling to Bronson was a new note sounding in the speeches and writings of the Messiah. He had missed it at first, perhaps in his turmoil over the fight he had with Helen. Whatever the case, he realized that he had never heard Franco Macalousso utter the name of Jesus. Except to call Him the Great Deceiver. Or the "One who came before." Yet he had never actually said Jesus' name.

This refusal to name Jesus might have to do with his utter contempt for a false Messiah. Yet there was something more troubling. A true Messiah could only be sent by God. He would be God's emissary on earth, the person who would usher in the kingdom that Jesus discussed thirty-seven times in the synoptic Gospels, according to one of Edna Williams's study guides.

More important, the Bible said that each time the name of Jesus was spoken, it had a power that neither Satan nor the Antichrist could match. If Franco Macalousso was, as Helen believed, the Antichrist, that would account for his fear of naming his enemy.

Bronson also noticed Macalousso's limited references to faith in God. Jesus certainly confronted all manner of horrors but never forgot where praise was due. The new Messiah spoke only of himself and the power within each person. He never reminded the world to love God before all else, an admonition as old as time, etched in stone from Exodus, and referred to again and again for eons.

And why would the real Messiah worry about such things as WNN's daily operations, its programming, and its ability to reach the world? Why would the real Messiah micromanage every aspect of the communications industry? Maybe there was something to what Helen had been trying to show him. Maybe . . .

"Good morning, Bronson. Mr. Parker wants to see you right away," said the floor director, when the new man arrived for work the morning after his confrontation with Helen.

In a short time, Len Parker had gone from being an observer to an unquestionable power and authority. He was acting as censor in a manner totally inappropriate for a respected broadcast facility such as WNN. Another troubling development.

As Bronson headed toward Parker's office, a young woman dressed in the uniform of a security officer brought a stack of papers to him. "Here's today's copy, Mr. Pearl," she said.

"Thanks, Kerry. But why the new look?" he asked.

"It was Mr. Parker's idea," she replied. "He wants the staff to show their faith in the Messiah. I feel a little silly, but if it proves my loyalty, that's okay with me."

Bronson shrugged, flipping through the notes as he continued down the hall.

Parker was sitting behind a large desk with several pieces of specialized equipment on it including a small television/VCR combination, three different tape recorders, a computer terminal, and several other electronic devices Bronson did not recognize. There was also a small stack of folders from the personnel office. Parker was reading Helen Hannah's file as Bronson entered the room and looked up, scowling.

"Trouble in Paradise, Len?" Bronson asked facetiously. He had seen Len Parker's type before, the type of man who gained his self-respect by attaching himself to a rising leader, his future, his self-esteem, all tied to the success or failure of that person. Such men could be ruthless, but Bronson found them to be pathetic cowards, grown-up versions of schoolyard bullies.

"Where's Miss Hannah, Mr. Pearl?" Parker asked coldly.

"How should I know?" Bronson shot back.

Parker rose from his desk, his body tensed and his suit jacket pulled back to reveal a side arm. He moved to the door, closed it, and said angrily, "Cut the bull, Pearl. Where is she?"

"I told you, I don't know," said Bronson, just as firmly.

Parker returned to his desk and switched on a micro-cassette tape recorder. He pressed the play button, surprising Bronson with the sound of his own voice. "I'm not saying there's nothing to it," he was saying. "My father spent every day of his life believing it. It made him a happier man. Maybe it even made him a better man. But at the end of the day, he still ended up dead, just like all of us will."

"His earthly body may have died, Bronson," Helen was heard to say, "but his soul is still very much alive."

"I wish I could believe that, Helen. Honest to God I do."

Parker stopped the tape and stared at Bronson. The journalist had been in dangerous situations before and always understood the risks of what he was doing. But this

time Bronson realized he was out of control. He was a surveillance target and even worse, Helen was involved.

"So just what do you believe, Mr. Pearl?" asked Parker.

"You've got the tape," he snapped back. "For all I know
you've got pictures too. You figure it out."

"Haven't made a decision about the Deceiver and the
Messiah?" Parker probed.

"Look," replied Bronson, "I walked out on the woman
I love. If you have the tape, you know that. That should tell
you what I believe."

"Not good enough, Mr. Pearl. A lover's quarrel is not a
theological difference. We need to know that you support
our Messiah."

"I'm sure not here because I support you," Bronson
angrily replied.

Len Parker refused to rise to the bait. He knew Bronson
was trying to change the subject, to avoid answering the
critical question.

"Helen Hannah's missing, Mr. Pearl," he continued.
Her car is parked near the apartment of Edna Williams, but
she's no longer there. We just hope she's not going to do
anything stupid." He paused, looking grimly at Bronson,
then added, "And put herself in danger."

"By danger, I assume you mean from yourself, right?"
said Bronson, his temper rising.

Parker shrugged. "It's my job to protect the interests of
the Messiah and the peace and unity he has brought to the
world. Hatred is the enemy now. I'll do whatever it takes to

eliminate every source of resistance. Obviously, when someone as prominent as Miss Hannah is against us, she has to be stopped for her own good and that of society."

"From what I've seen the hatred is coming from zealots like you," Bronson shot back. "It's the extremists who are defacing churches and attacking Christians. I've heard that term before, Parker. Sometimes they call it ethnic cleansing. Sometimes they call it reeducation. But murder is more to the point, isn't it? You're going to kill Helen and anyone who shares her beliefs, aren't you?"

"Look, Mr. Pearl," Parker replied calmly, "I'm not Ms. Hannah's enemy. I'm just trying to serve the Messiah and bring peace and unity to the world. Who could possibly have a problem with that?"

"Said the spider to the fly . . . ," mumbled Bronson, turning and leaving the office. For the first time he realized that Helen might have a point. But where was she? Where was Helen?

∽

The agent was startled by the ringing telephone. The apartment was empty; the woman who had once lived there was among the vanished and the telephone seemed like a voice rising from the grave. Three rings. Four rings. "Peace in the name of the Lord," said a voice on the answering machine. "This is Edna Williams. Please leave your name, telephone number, and a brief message. And rejoice in this day that the Lord has made."

"Helen? Are you there? Please pick up the phone. You must be there, Helen? Helen?" The agent recognized the voice of Bronson Pearl. So it was true, he really didn't know where she was.

It would be useful information for Commander Parker as he continued his search of the apartment.

Chapter 17

LEN PARKER SENSED that he had to move quickly. His faith in the Messiah was such that he could not imagine anyone not sharing his commitment, but unfortunately there were extremists loose and it was his job to take care of them, which was the reason he was talking with the newsroom director in the control booth. "I understand that you're the guy who can help me," he said. "I have a concern that someone might say something damaging on the air, something that might slow down the work we're doing. I'm sure we all want to avoid such an eventuality."

"I'm surprised you're worried," replied the director. "You've watched our feeds from around the world. Everyone is happy now. We have peace. Real peace. I don't think any comment from a Hater is going to change that."

"Probably not," Parker agreed, "but with all the Messiah has done for us, I don't want to risk causing him pain. Are we protected with our broadcasts?"

"A little," the director explained, "though I think you'll probably want to go to a twelve-second delay system rather than the five-second one we have now. That way you'll have twelve seconds to review every transmission before it gets sent out. If anyone says something harmful, you simply preempt the transmission. We do it on live call-in shows all the time."

Parker was pleased. "Good, set it up and make certain I can monitor it from my office, but don't mention this to anyone. We don't want them thinking we're worried about the Haters."

"Consider it done, Mr. Parker," said the director.

That evening's newscast was Bronson's first since Helen's disappearance, and he and the director agreed to go with the standard intro, "Across America and around the world, you're watching WNN with Bronson Pearl and Helen Hannah."

Bronson smiled into the camera. "Good evening. I'm Bronson Pearl. Helen Hannah is on special assignment. As the situation in Europe and the Middle East continues to improve, President Macalousso has been meeting with world leaders in Bonn, Germany, and an announcement is expected any time now. Of course, we'll bring that to you live when it happens. Right now, with more on this situation in Bonn, is WNN German correspondent Samantha Metcalfe."

The screen switched to a reporter standing in front of a government building. "It has now been confirmed that foreign ministers from the European Union, as well as leading religious dignitaries from around the world, have been meeting all night in this German government building," she reported. "The attendees began arriving late last evening at the request of the man who is now familiar to the entire planet."

The screen next showed earlier footage of a press conference being held by two men, an Islamic extremist, and a Jewish rabbi. The Islamic leader spoke first.

"We have all seen remarkable events occur over the past several days," he said. "Clearly our entire world has undergone an extraordinary change. The planet being saved from almost certain destruction, and the Haters of peace and unity have been removed, but the most incredible sign has been the realization by the entire world that President Franco Macalousso is indeed the Messiah he claims to be. He is walking among us, living as one of us, bringing us the fulfillment of prophecy."

"More will be revealed within a few days," the rabbi added. "For now, the first issue we had to resolve was how to recognize the true Messiah. He would bring peace. Did Jesus bring peace? No. Only the true Messiah did that."

A quick cut back to the studio showed Bronson looking into the camera. "I have just received word that we're ready to go live to the embassy in Bonn. Apparently an agreement has been reached. Samantha?"

"This is an exciting moment for the world, Bronson," the reporter said. "You can see for yourself what just happened. A leader of the Arab world and a leader of Israel have just shook hands, indicating a final peace agreement has been reached. We have been told that there will be an address by President Macalousso in a few minutes."

There was a hush among the gathered reporters as a spokesman stepped to the microphone and cleared his throat. "I am pleased to announce that the Messiah has achieved something today that no man has ever been able to do before. He has brokered a full and comprehensive Middle East peace agreement. This seven-year, far-reaching agreement goes well beyond a simple peace between Arabs and Jews. It involves all the major leaders of the world, establishing a newly agreed-upon constitution for Planet Earth." Reporters began shouting as the spokesman held up his hands. "I'm afraid I can't tell you anything more at the moment. President Macalousso will be talking with you shortly, and at that time he will be able to answer your questions."

In the studio, Bronson Pearl was startled by the suddenness of the breaking news. Normally when a major event took place, reporters were briefed in advance to prepare their commentary and analysis.

"You have heard the announcement," Bronson told his audience, "a seven-year peace treaty in the Middle East brokered by President Macalousso. When we return, we'll talk to our chief political correspondent in Washington to get his take on these startling events. We'll also, of course, carry President Macalousso's address live."

Bronson smiled into the camera as he remembered what Helen had shown him about the seven-year treaty. Increasingly he thought she might be right, and while he still did not understand the miracles he had witnessed, he was beginning to believe that Franco Macalousso was not all he claimed to be.

∽

Helen Hannah thought she was being cautious when she left her grandmother's house. She did know that her actions were not going to be popular and, to stay inconspicuous, she would have to abandon her car. Since she made her decision to leave, the WNN markings on her car would become an easy way to spot her. Helen walked the first several blocks into Midtown. She had earlier watched the newscast Bronson was anchoring. Surely, she thought, he understood now. The announcement of a seven-year treaty had to shock him into reality. She missed him, wanted to see and talk to him and hold him, desperately needing him to understand the truth, to grasp what she had been saying. "God, please show me what to do," she prayed. She made her way back to WNN, entering the parking garage where Bronson's four-wheel-drive SUV was kept. They had long since traded keys to each other's vehicles, and she opened his door and placed a large brown envelope on the passenger seat.

What she hadn't realized was that a tracking sensor had activated a small alarm in Len Parker's office when she entered Bronson's car. He was certain she was one of the Haters, a follower of the Deceiver who could not be threatened, and would have to be eliminated. Ironically, Bronson Pearl had prepared the viewing audience for her death by telling them she was on special assignment. It would be easy to create a story where she became the news herself, her death declared a great tragedy at the height of a brilliant career.

Helen, relying on her professional instincts, realized she was being followed. Two figures were watching her down the city streets. Helen had spent enough time as a general-assignment reporter to understand the rhythm of the streets at all hours of the day and night and was familiar with the myriad alleys that honeycombed the metropolis.

She turned onto the first side street she approached and began running. Even as she heard a vehicle stop, its doors open, and the voices of her pursuers behind her, she flattened herself to the ground, covering her body with trash to blend in with her surroundings. In the dim light of a street lamp, she was perfectly camouflaged and, not hearing her chasers, she felt safe breaking cover. Slowly standing up she moved stealthily before a pair of hands grabbed her. Before she could cry out, her assailant pulled her arm backward, forcing her to the ground. Two more hands grabbed Helen's free arm, bringing her other wrist back as she felt cold handcuffs being clamped on. "If you yell, we'll Mace you," one of her assailants warned. "You're coming with us, and any further resistance is just going to get you hurt."

Chapter 18

BRONSON PEARL WAS ANGRY AND CONFUSED. The more he thought about what he had seen and heard, the more puzzling it seemed.

First came the event that had to be the Rapture, at least as Helen explained it and as the Bible had confirmed. Too many good people had disappeared. Too many of those left behind contradicted Macalousso's explanation of what had happened.

Then there was the incident with the missiles and the hostile armies, the advent of instant peace in the midst of what appeared to be total war. Surely this was the warrior king so many people believed would be the Messiah. Jesus was the Good Shepherd, killed for the sins of the world, yet the army of the Caesars continued conquering for many years after His death on the cross. Yet Macalousso would not speak the name of Jesus, and hadn't the Bible discussed the power of that name over all the evil of the world?

But, thought Bronson angrily. *I just can't believe that the prophets of the Old Testament could see into the future.*

I can't believe that whoever wrote the book of Revelation knew what our lives would be like today.

As he opened the car door, he noticed the envelope containing a Gideon Bible and a single cassette tape. He knew that Helen must have placed the envelope there, although there was no writing on the cassette and no label. Putting it in his player, he began listening as he drove.

An announcer's voice began, "You're listening to *Point of View* on the USA Radio Network." This was followed by someone named Marlin Maddoux, whom Bronson had never heard of.

"Welcome to *Point of View*. I'm Marlin Maddoux. Today we're talking about one of the questions that every Christian asks at one time or another. If God really exists, then why doesn't He simply show Himself to the world? He's God. He can do anything He wants. Right? Well, today we're going to answer that very question by talking about one of the most important elements of the Christian experience, faith. Faith is what lets us know in our hearts that even long after our loved ones may have departed, their spirit still lives forever in the presence of the Lord. As the Bible says, 'Absent from the body, present with the Lord.'"

Bronson, listening intently, touched the rewind button and replayed the words, ". . . long after our loved ones may have departed, their spirit still lives forever in the presence of the Lord."

He slowed, turned his truck around on the dark road, and picked up speed rapidly. It was almost one in the morning before Bronson reached the cemetery. The big iron gates were locked, but he was able to slip through a break in the fence, taking a small penlight from his glove compartment to light the familiar grounds and finally stopping by a headstone that read: JAMES STEVEN PEARL 1929–1991. Below that was a Scripture reference, 1 Thessalonians 4:16–17. Dropping to one knee, he brushed some dirt from the stone, and sadly said, "Hi, Dad."

Suddenly Bronson felt awkward. He needed to talk to his father about the Bible, about faith. As he sat staring at the grave barely illuminated by the quarter moon in the cloudy night, he murmured, "What was it, Dad? What made you decide with all your heart to believe? You never saw in your whole lifetime what I've seen in the past week. This Macalousso guy is . . . well, he's the real thing, Dad. He must be. I saw him. I saw him do things no one could possibly do. He's done things not even Jesus could do. He's brought peace to the whole world. Just about the whole world believes everything this guy says, and my mind tells me they're right to do so. But in my heart . . ." He paused and swallowed hard.

"I don't really believe, Dad. I don't know if it's the discernment you always talked about or if I'm just a cynic. All I know is that something's holding me back. I can't explain it, but it's something that keeps tugging at me. Helen's part of it. She's convinced he's evil. She calls him the Antichrist and keeps showing me books and tapes and Bible passages that support her position. And she may be right. But there's something else. Something . . ." Tears began to stream down Bronson's face. He realized that this was the first open, honest, heartfelt conversation he had ever held with his father. "Oh God, Dad! I wish you were here with me now. I know you'd know what to say. You always did. I just didn't know how to listen."

Bronson touched the tombstone, a cold slab of marble offering no comfort. Yet even as he touched the smooth material, the moonlight momentarily broke through the clouds, falling on the grave. JAMES STEVEN PEARL 1929–1991. 1 Thessalonians 4:16–17.

It was the Bible verse that caught Bronson's attention. His father's will requested the verse be part of the memorial, but he had long forgotten the particular words. Sensing it was suddenly vital to understand what his father was trying to tell, he hurriedly returned to his car and opened the Bible and read, "For the Lord himself shall descend from heaven with a shout, with the voice of the archangel, and with the trump of God: and the dead in Christ shall rise first: Then we which are alive and remain shall be caught up together with them in the clouds to meet the Lord in the air: and so shall we ever be with the Lord."

Bronson sat for a moment, rereading the verse, thinking. Helen Hannah's grandmother had been one of the raptured. Between her leaving and the material she left behind, Helen had all the proof she needed about God, Jesus, and Macalousso.

Bronson was different. He understood Helen's emotions,

yet he also accepted the potential validity of Macalousso's claims.

But the real answer lay with the dead, those who offered no threat to Macalousso, and no reason to be afraid.

There was a portable shovel among his other emergency equipment in the back of the truck. He took it out and went back to the grave.

The work was difficult. The shovel, a two-piece unit, was sturdy but not designed for heavy use. He had to force the blade into the ground, but fortunately the earth was soft, and he moved quickly.

"Lord, if this is sinful, please understand," he prayed. "I have to know. I have to see for myself. The story I have to tell is important."

His shoes and pants were mud-covered and his shirt was covered with sweat by the time Bronson's shovel at last hit the lid of the casket.

"Dad, I don't know if I want you to be in there or not," he said as he cleared away the dirt. "Yet if Helen is right, I have nothing to fear."

But Bronson was frightened, saying words to avoid the action he now had to take. "Lord, give me strength," he said, forcing open the coffin.

The first thing he saw was the suit. "My Sunday best," his father had called it. The last time Bronson had seen the suit, it covered his father's remains. Now it lay at the bottom of the empty coffin, looking as though it was waiting to be put back on the rack.

A wedding ring, Timex watch, and a thin gold chain with a small cross on it were on top of the clothes. There was also an open Bible, facedown in the coffin. Bronson picked up the book and propped his flashlight in the dirt, letting the light fall on the page. It was opened to 1 Corinthians 15, with several sentences highlighted by the yellow marker his father always carried with him. "For the trumpet shall sound, and the dead shall be raised . . . Death is swallowed up in victory. O death, where is thy sting? O grave, where is thy victory?"

And then he knew. Not in his mind, but in his heart. Bronson Pearl, for the first time in his life, understood the truth, the joy of the people the Antichrist called the Haters. Now he believed. His father was not lost. Helen's grandmother was not lost. One had died. One had been raptured. But they were all together. And though he had been left behind, though he knew there would be a time of trial where he would have to confront evil, victory would ultimately be won by the Lord. Of that he was certain, and it was a faith he would profess to his death if it came to that.

Chapter

AS TIME PASSED the public's perception of Franco Macalousso began to change. The rejoicing continued, even as families tried to come to grips with the loss of those who had disappeared. But the horror of chaos and destruction had faded. Peace was in the land, and people gradually returned to the familiar patterns of life.

In the WNN studios, Len Parker sensed a problem as he watched the latest speech from Macalousso, taped for later broadcast, to allow him to fine-tune the recorded images.

"Hold it," commanded Parker to the editor. "Freeze it there." Macalousso's appeal came from the excitement people felt witnessing him in person, walking through throngs to reach the podium. But now there was less appeal. They understood the Messiah was in their midst, but the novelty had worn thin.

This latest speech was proof, with a crowd befitting a minor celebrity, but one not worthy of the true Messiah. "Fix that crowd," Parker ordered. "You've got some earlier footage. Edit in more people."

Suddenly the sound of a woman's voice broke into his troubled thoughts. "So even God needs your electronic enhancement?" he heard Helen Hannah say.

She walked into the room, her handcuffed wrists locked behind her back. The agent was holding her arm, but she made no move to resist. "You don't think he can convince the world of who he is without your editing people into a crowd scene?" she asked.

"I see your version of God didn't do much to help you." Parker smirked. "Or is a miracle going to break those handcuffs?" Turning to the agent he ordered, "Take her to my office. I'll be right there."

Inside Parker's office, no effort was made to remove the handcuffs and make Helen more comfortable. They wanted her to be constantly reminded of who she was and how her life was now in their hands.

"You've got no idea what you're up against, Ms. Hannah," began Parker.

"I have a better idea than you think, and I'm not afraid of you," she shot back.

"Well, you should be! Don't mistake our talk of peace and unity for weakness. People want peace at any price, and we will give it to them. They want to believe that they are more than just flesh and blood, and we'll tell them they are. But we're not fools."

"I think the serpent did the same thing in the Garden of Eden," replied Helen.

"Child's play, Miss Hannah," responded Parker. "What

we have done is beyond anything written in the Bible. Our Messiah is real."

"You mean Franco Macalousso?" asked Helen. "And if they don't worship him?"

"Then they die," was his chilling answer. "You have never seen the wrathful side of Franco Macalousso. Do you really understand what he's capable of? You worship him or you die a death more horrible than you could ever imagine." Turning to the agent, he said, "Take her away."

᠃

It was evening when Franco Macalousso made his next speech, deliberately timed to be seen by the largest number of people. The crowd in the stadium topped one hundred thousand standing shoulder to shoulder. Yet, unlike the first speech, the number watching the big-screen, closed-circuit broadcasts had dropped. The WNN cameras broadcast enhanced images, a thousand people were transformed into ten thousand, and a hundred people were made to look like a sea of eager faces. It was the magic of television, and it was effective.

"Today is your day!" announced Macalousso. "I will show you wonders beyond anything you have ever imagined. I will lead you into a whole new world of human possibility. In this new world you will discover the powers of divinity buried deep in your soul. But we must be together, as a single entity. Even though I have removed the tares from the wheat, there are still those among you who have chosen not to join us. They have become cancer cells in our body, and until they have been removed, we cannot take the next step into godhood. They are standing in your way."

The crowds listened, spellbound, to a message that asked little but promised much. They had long hoped there had to be more to life than the challenges of the Bible. Now they knew: they, too, were gods. They had only to rid the world of the Haters and their rightful inheritance would be handed over. They would have powers and abilities beyond their wildest dreams.

As the speech ended, the people moved into the streets, quickly becoming a mob. "Are you a Hater?" they asked passersby. "Do you accept Macalousso as your lord and savior? Will you destroy those who stand in the way of our blessed destiny?"

Any excuse was greeted with derision, and violence invariably ensued. Some were beaten to death, and one victim had his necktie used as a garrote and his corpse lifted onto a telephone pole as an example to others.

WNN reporters in the field tried to make sense of what was taking place just outside the stadium. Excited followers were singing, praying, and praising Macalousso, but there was also an undercurrent of anger.

"These Haters think they can put themselves ahead of the whole world," said one man to a reporter. "Look at the promise that has been made. We can gain the godhood if we rid the land of this handful of rebels."

"I can hardly wait for the fulfillment of the promise," echoed a woman who had stopped to listen to the interview. "The Messiah says that we're all gods. He says that we have great powers within us all. We've got to do whatever it takes to get rid of the Haters who are standing in our way."

The mob scenes were just the reaction Macalousso had desired as a cover for solidifying his power by terror, or even elimination, of the new Christians.

For the event, WNN was given exclusive rights, with Len Parker handpicking the reporters who would handle the coverage. "The Messiah wants this to be a coordinated effort," he explained. "The footage shot by WNN will be made available to all other television networks. We can't risk the reporters' lives if the Haters become violent and try to retaliate."

⋄⋄

Bronson Pearl's body ached. He had been awake for thirty hours and knew his reflexes were dull and his thoughts not as clear as they should be. What mattered was getting away from New York, from the WNN headquarters and Len Parker.

As thorough as the Macalousso organization might be, they had been in power less than a week. They didn't grasp the complexities of the regional bureaus, where the most-respected professionals were given deference.

Driving to Boston, Bronson told the WNN bureau that he had been assigned to handle some fieldwork, and would need a camera crew and a satellite link so he could go live with a commentary.

As the global violence escalated, Bronson sat in the satellite uplink truck, watching the monitor, waiting for the moment when he could tap into every station in the world-wide network. As he waited, he watched with horror at the scenes unfolding around the world.

From Toronto several soldiers wearing bulletproof vests and carrying high-powered handguns and potent chemical sprays used a battering ram to break down a door. It was smashed easily and the camera stayed with the soldiers as they rushed from room to room, pausing just long enough to make certain no one was waiting in ambush. Finally they reached the first bedroom and the camera paused briefly on a sign reading, "Shhh. Child of God, beloved of Jesus, sleeping here." The soldiers crashed into the room and the men grabbed a small child from his bed, one rip-ping a cross from the wall and holding it long enough for the cameraman to get a close-up of it being crushed under his boot.

In Miami, a camera equipped with night vision revealed a man in a second-story apartment, holding a small child and lowering him into the waiting arms of a woman standing in the shadows of the alley below. The woman caught the child, easing him to the ground. But as she looked up for her second baby, she was grabbed, forced to the ground, and handcuffed. In the apartment above, the remaining child was ripped from the arms of his father, who was struck down with the butt of a pistol. A moment later, the family was reunited in the front of the building, the man's jaw broken and his face covered with blood. The children were crying, reaching for their parents but restrained by other soldiers, and the woman, her hands cuffed behind her back, was held by her hair, her face forced upward, as her neighbors jeered, ridiculed, and spat at her.

The soldiers ignored the woman's pleas to take her children to the home of a friend. "They're not Haters," she begged. "They believe in the Messiah. Please let my children go."

The soldiers forced the couple into one patrol car, the children in another. As the cars moved down the streets, the neighbors cheered, praising Macalousso.

There were other scenes, other arrests. In Minneapolis, a mob attacked a secret religious bookstore. In Los Angeles, Bibles were removed from churches, transported to MacArthur Park, covered with gasoline, and ignited.

Other burnings took place in Tokyo, Pretoria, Hong Kong, Rome, São Paulo, Paris, and elsewhere. One reporter exclaimed on camera, "It's truly ironic that the very Book that once divided the world is now bringing it together."

It was late morning before the violence was finally over, the flames doused, and the arrested moved to holding camps. On an isolated hill overlooking the bay, Bronson Pearl stood alone, microphone in hand, speaking into the camera. "Don't worry about the timing," Bronson told the technician in the satellite uplink truck. "Just use my code when you send this and they'll cut into the broadcast to carry me live. It's a system we use when we've got a breaking story. They'll understand in New York." *No reason to alert them to my actions,* he added silently.

The camera operator adjusted the lens, took a sound level, then signaled the reporter to begin. Bronson looked into the camera. "I'm Bronson Pearl, and for those of you who have watched my broadcasts over the years, you know that I've always told you the truth as I knew it. I was called the most trusted man in American broadcasting a few weeks ago, and while I'm not certain I deserve that title, I have never gone on the air without first checking all the facts. I was in the valley of Armageddon when the war we so desperately feared began. I was present when President Macalousso arrived, and I witnessed firsthand the vanishing of the weapons of mass destruction. I heard him declare himself Messiah, and I've seen the wonders he has performed. I have also investigated him thoroughly, which is why I'm reporting to you tonight. Franco Macalousso is *not* the Messiah. He has not returned to save the planet from evil. Quite the opposite is true. Franco Macalousso is the embodiment of evil itself. He is the one the Bible calls the Antichrist. I have always told you the truth. That is why I'm asking you today to please listen to what I am saying. Do you think a Messiah would fear a book such as the Bible? Of course not. But he has ordered the burning of every book that tells the truth. The Bibles do not promote hatred as he would have you believe. The Bibles tell the truth about God, about the real Messiah, and about the ultimate evil of the Antichrist, President Macalousso."

∽

"Cut!" screamed Len Parker. "How did that Hater preempt our broadcast?"

"The patch code was used to signal a breaking story," came the explanation from a bystander. "That takes precedence over anything else on the air."

"How dare he pull a stunt like this," bellowed Parker. "I'll have him killed."

The men and women in the room stared in shock. Some were angry with Bronson for denouncing the Messiah. Some were angry with Parker. Most were confused. And a few, who had been nodding their heads with what they were hearing, quietly went back to work, saying nothing.

∽

Bronson was certain his broadcast would be stopped, but there was no way of knowing exactly when. He continued talking even as he heard sirens approaching in the distance. He continued as the police cars screeched to a halt and a dozen guards rushed over to him. He continued as they grabbed him, slamming the microphone to the ground, and shoved him into the backseat of a patrol car.

Chapter 20

THE "SPONTANEOUS" CELEBRATIONS had been ordered by Franco Macalousso as part of a worldwide recognition of his ascendancy as Messiah. Government offices and schools were closed. Businesses were ordered to let their employees off, and billboards, banners, and signs flashed photos of Macalousso and proclaimed, "He's back!" and "The Messiah Is Here."

In contrast to the celebrations, there were other less joyous events taking place. The number of Hater arrests was growing beyond anyone's expectations, local jails and prisons filling to capacity. College dorms, stadiums, and open fields throughout the country became makeshift prisons, encircled with razor wire and using officers with attack dogs to patrol the perimeter.

The first goal was reeducation with giant television monitors wired throughout these crude prisons and WNN broadcasts shown throughout the day and night of the Messiah, taped programs, special speeches, and group counseling sessions. Those people who finally understood

Macalousso's version of the truth would be returned to society. The remainder would be killed like a cancer cut away by a surgeon. The Messiah himself believed that all but a handful among the Haters would have to die.

Vans and police cruisers were originally used, but these proved too limited. Commandeering city buses to transport the haters to these "reeducation centers" was suggested but had been vetoed by the Messiah. Too many buses would cripple public transportation and people would want to know why. Cattle trucks were used instead, the prisoners riding standing up, their bodies pressed together, to allow the maximum number per vehicle.

The New York holding facility was approximately forty miles outside of Manhattan in the stadium of a large community college. Women were separated from men, children from parents. Isolation, fear, and worry kept the crowds docile.

As soon as he arrived, Bronson spotted Helen among the women being taken to the processing area, and he hurried to her side, taking her hand as she stood in line. "I should never have doubted your courage," she told him. "I didn't see your broadcast, but the women who were just brought in talk of nothing else. They praise the Lord for your bravery."

"I have the awful feeling that all I did was assure my arrest," mused Bronson.

"It doesn't matter," replied Helen. "The Lord knows what was in your heart."

"Break it up, you two!" shouted one of the guards. "This

isn't the nightly news. You, Hannah, stay with the women. As for you, Pearl . . ." He reached out and poked Bronson in the stomach with an electric cattle prod, and mocked him as he groaned in pain.

"Bronson Pearl, the most trusted journalist in America. I hereby dub you King of the Haters!" He jolted him again, this time on the head, and the newsman fell to the ground in agony.

"You're going to kill him!" shouted Helen from across the yard. She started to run but was grabbed, handcuffed, and then chained to a post in the women's section.

"Don't worry. We're not going to kill him," chided one of the guards. "That would spoil the fun we have planned."

Len Parker had been ordered to the prison where Helen and Bronson were being kept to assure total security. The Messiah was now using WNN extensively, and he did not want any surprises from the Haters. The two most important voices on the network would face their punishment in prime time. For his followers, it would be an occasion for joy. For the hidden Christians, it would be a warning to change their ways or suffer the same fate.

In the warden's office of the makeshift prison camp, the television was tuned constantly to WNN. As Parker arrived, the announcer was saying, "Every word out of the Messiah's mouth is both glorious and vital, but tonight's message promises to be the most moving of all. Not only will he continue his outpouring of love to every corner of the globe, he will also guide us to godhood."

Parker had ignored the speech, standing by the window as the cattle trucks arrived, each unloading more and more of the followers of the Deceiver.

"There are more of these Haters than any of us dared to believe," he said. "If they keep pouring in like this, I don't know how we're going to process them all."

But, even as he spoke, he knew that ultimately this was not about reeducation. The new followers of the Deceiver had come to see the raptured as proof of the truth of the Bible. They would happily go to their deaths before renouncing Jesus.

It was the ones who remained undecided, who had heard enough rumors to question the Messiah but were not yet committed to the Deceiver, who needed to be convinced. *Maybe once they see their beloved Bronson Pearl executed on national television, they'll take a step back,* Parker thought. *If they'd rather die than worship the Messiah . . . well, that's their choice. But make no mistake, we will crush anyone who stands in our way.*

In the holding area, a loudspeaker broadcast the new speech by Macalousso while an elderly woman sat on the ground, her head down as if sleeping.

"This is a day of unity, of love, and of peace," said the amplified voice of Macalousso. "It is time for you to join me as I show you the way of total surrender."

"Hey, what is that old woman doing?" demanded one of the guards watching with binoculars from the top of the stadium.

"Sleeping, it looks like," said a second, straining to see.

"Her lips are moving, and the way she's holding her hands . . . ," the first guard replied. "Radio down there to check her out."

"It was written long ago that God is love," said Macalousso's voice. "Have I not shown you great love?"

"It's a Bible," the radio crackled, as guards raced over to the old woman, grabbing the small book from her hands and tearing out the pages. She was hauled roughly to her feet. "That should have been burned before you got here," they shouted. "How'd you hide it?"

The woman was silent.

"I want this one taken to the infirmary and strip-searched to see what else she's hiding," the commander ordered.

The guard put the woman in a painful wrist hold, dragging her toward one of the exits. Another prisoner tried to stop him and another guard rushed over, striking him with the butt of a rifle, dislocating his jaw, and sending him sprawling to the ground.

". . . Do you not feel a new love burning in your hearts?" Macalousso continued. "A new love for life and for each other? That is the love of God. And I can give it to you, for I am the Lord."

જી

It was nightfall when the guards forced the prisoners back into the cattle cars that had brought them to the stadium.

There were hundreds of new Christians being held, and they greatly outnumbered the soldiers. If there was a riot, they might have even gained control of the holding area, which was why Parker insisted they be caged during the hanging of Bronson Pearl.

There was no time to build a proper gallows, but a less sophisticated version had the same results. A noose had been rigged between two cattle cars, and a camera placed to record the event as the trapped prisoners watched helplessly.

"Hey, Pearl, ready to show the world what kind of hero you really are?" shouted one of the guards as he opened the stepladder for Bronson to stand for his execution.

"Get ready to meet that God of yours, Pearl," taunted another guard. "Mine's already down here with me."

The men who were crowded together with Bronson were silent. Some were praying, others were trying to find words of comfort while a few wept openly, unsure whether their tears were for God, Bronson, or themselves.

"Hey, it's okay, you guys," said the condemned man. "Our hope is not in this world. Never has been. So I'm leaving this place a little earlier than I planned. At least I know the truth I was once too blind to see. We should thank God for giving us all a second chance."

"Amen," said one voice. "Praise the Lord," said another. "Amen to that." "Thank You, Jesus."

Len Parker and several guards walked to the truck where four men positioned themselves, two on each side of the door, their automatic weapons pointed at the prisoners as two other guards opened the door.

The door opened and two guards roughly pulled Bronson from the truck. One of them kicked him in the back of the knees and knocked him to the ground. His wrists were bound behind his back, and he was pulled to his feet and dragged toward the gallows.

Inside one of the women's trucks, Helen watched with horror. She knew she should not have waited so long to tell Bronson she would marry him. Her grandmother had been right. Now her grandmother was gone, and soon . . .

One of the other women began singing "Because He Lives," her voice growing louder and bolder. By the time she reached the chorus, others in the holding yard had joined in. Len Parker was livid, yet there was nothing he could do short of killing them all, and mass murder for the moment would have to wait.

Bronson looked over to Helen, their eyes meeting. Their love for each other was like a spark jumping between them. As Bronson was forced up the small stepladder, the noose placed around his neck, he heard Helen scream, "No! No! You can't do this!"

"But we can," said Parker. "Tonight is the ultimate ratings test. From what I hear, the death of Bronson Pearl will win its time slot with a bigger audience than the Olympics. In fact, we just might make this a two-night event."

"Our hope is not in *this* world, Parker," she replied.

Parker turned to the guard who was to kick the ladder

from under Bronson. "Just a few seconds more. The Messiah said to wait exactly for midnight."

On one wall of the holding area, a giant-screen television showed a close-up of Bronson, his neck in the noose, an image that was being broadcast around the world.

"Twenty seconds to go," said Parker. "Nineteen. Eighteen. Seventeen."

Suddenly Bronson's voice could be heard. "I'm Bronson Pearl, and for those of you who have watched my broadcasts over the years, you know that I've always told you the truth as I knew it." The voice was coming from the monitor speaker and Parker looked up in horror, watching a repeat of Bronson's last broadcast.

"Who in hell put that into the broadcast feed?" he shrieked.

"I was in the valley of Armageddon when the war we all so desperately feared began," Bronson continued. "I was present when President Macalousso arrived."

"Somebody get through to New York," Parker shouted. "Find out what's going on. Tell the guards to kill anyone they see. Tell the guards . . ." Parker halted, realizing he was powerless.

At that moment Bronson began to lose his balance. "Grab him!" shouted Parker. "Don't let him die until the whole world is watching. The Messiah has ordered it."

"Franco Macalousso is *not* the Messiah," Bronson was saying. "He has not returned to save the planet from evil."

One of the guards grabbed Bronson, forcing him back

on the ladder. As a precaution, he took off the noose but left his wrists still bound.

"President Macalousso is the Antichrist. He is not who he says he is," Bronson's voice thundered.

"The twelve-second delay," shouted Parker. "There's supposed to be a twelve-second delay."

"President Macalousso is the Antichrist." The words echoed.

In the WNN control room, an agent sat smiling, looking at the two Parker guards he had handcuffed and gagged on the floor in front of him. "You men didn't go through the academy, did you?" he asked. They stared at him, silent, unable to reply.

"One of the things they taught us was to understand a man's weakness," the agent continued. He paused, listening to Bronson's comments being broadcast to every part of the world. "Some fears are justified, of course," the mysterious man continued. "But some fears reveal a weakness you can use. A man might be afraid of the dark, so you know you should plan your attack by night. And so we come to Franco Macalousso, this self-proclaimed Messiah."

The guards looked startled. This agent had been one of the inner circle.

"I have known Franco Macalousso from the beginning," he said. "I witnessed the miracles, and yes, I do believe they were miracles. One day I'll ask the real Messiah how it happened, but I guess we have a few years until that happens." He smiled. "I can see by your eyes that you have questions. Well, come to our Father's house and hopefully you will understand. Do you know what Franco Macalousso's real weakness is, gentlemen? It's truth. He is the Antichrist, and as my late mother used to say when I was too stupid to get it, Jesus is Lord! Hallelujah!"

∽

Len Parker was terrified. He had lost all control of the events the Messiah had placed him in charge of. On the giant screen, he was watching a carefully made broadcast of audio and video material secretly recorded over the past few days. Only an insider with access to the tapes could have done it, and the only insider whose background included specialized electronic training was a certain agent back in New York. But there was no way . . .

Parker suddenly heard his own voice, recorded during the conversation with Helen Hannah. "Don't mistake our talk of peace and unity for weakness," he was saying.

Helen's voice came up loud and clear, "I think the serpent did the same thing in the Garden of Eden."

The damning conversation continued as security officers tried to break into the control room where the nameless agent was broadcasting.

The voices coming over the studio monitors began to drift over the prison camp. The image switched to a Jack Van Impe broadcast tape.

"True salvation and everlasting life are God's gift to everyone," the preacher said. "And all you have to do is ask

Him, with an open mind and an open heart. If you want Jesus to come into your life right now, then bow your heads and join me in praying the sinner's prayer."

In Mexico City, in a crowded cantina, several men watched a television screen. A few laughed derisively and one grabbed a handful of jalapêno peppers and hurled them at the screen. But off to the far end of the bar, a worker in worn coveralls and muddy boots, his face caked with dried sweat, set aside his beer, slid to his knees, and bowed his head in prayer.

Others from around the world joined the Mexican worker, together reciting along with Jack Van Impe, "Dear Lord, I know that I am a sinner. But please come into my life . . ."

Len Parker was screaming hysterically at the guards, trying to get them to turn off the monitor. He grabbed a rifle, aimed at the monitor, and began firing. It exploded and shards of glass littered the yard. But the sound continued from the speakers, the words of praise and truth unsilenced.

It was then that a light appeared, not lightning, though lightning was Parker's first thought when he saw the flash. It struck one of the cattle trucks with laserlike intensity and there was a crashing sound, which Parker realized was the giant door of the truck falling open.

"Shoot any hater who tries to escape!" he shouted, looking frantically for the traitor who had opened the door.

There was another flash and the second door crashed to

the ground as some of the prisoners began singing "Amazing Grace."

"Shut up!" screamed a guard holding a machine gun. "Shut up or I'll blow a hole in every last one of you."

Another flash struck the weapon. The guard screamed, dropping the machine gun, his hands suddenly blistered as though thrust into fire. The weapon lay on the grass, sizzling in the night dew.

The prisoners began filing from the trucks, moving quickly but no longer afraid. They would not die tonight. The time of trial was just beginning, of that they were sure. But they would endure because the Lord was with them. This was His battle, and He had triumphed.

Helen ran to Bronson and untied his wrists. They clung to one another as Len Parker rushed toward them, brandishing his rifle. One of the prisoners tackled him, knocking the gun from his hands, and dragged him into one of the cattle cars, his hands cuffed to the slats.

"You can't stop the inevitable!" Parker screamed. "You know that, don't you? There's nothing you can do to change the future."

Bronson and Helen walked over to him. "Come on, Len," Helen said. "I'm sure you read the Book. Didn't you get to the end? Your buddy's got a little time for bluster and parlor tricks. But he's the Antichrist. Don't you get it? He's in the Book. Jesus is in the book. In a sense, we're all in the Book. And you know what? No matter what you do. No matter what your false Messiah says, in the end, God wins!"

Before Parker could respond, a patrol car came racing onto the prison grounds, sirens blaring and lights flashing. It pulled to a stop in front of Helen and Bronson, the driver leaning across the seat to open the door. "Get in, you two," he said. "It took a miracle to get out here. I don't think I'm going to have another one tonight."

Helen, surprised, stared into the face of the mysterious agent.

"Yes, now will you get in?" he said, smiling. "I'm all alone here, and you remember what it says, 'wherever two or three are gathered in My name . . .'"

"Hallelujah," said Bronson, helping Hannah inside then closing the door as the car picked up speed. "I can't wait for Macalousso to hear about the ratings for tonight's broadcast."

FROM THE PRODUCERS OF LEFT BEHIND: THE MOVIE

Tribulation

Danger, intrigue, deception,
...welcome to the last days.

Surrounded by the love of his family, police detective Tom Canboro (Gary Busey) enjoys a rich and full life. But he finds himself battling more than thieves when he takes on a mysterious group that possesses frightening psychic powers. When his wife (Sherri Miller), sister (Margot Kidder), and brother in law (Howie Mandel) become the target of this dark society, he rushes to their aid. However, before he can reach them, a mystical force takes control of his car thrusting him headlong into the path of an oncoming truck.

Tom wakes up from a coma to find himself in a world that has undergone a frightening transformation. A self-proclaimed Messiah (Nick Mancuso) rules the world and almost everyone proudly supports a mark on their right hand signifying their allegiance to this global leader. Millions have simply disappeared, and no one left behind can remember that they even existed.

In a state of confusion, Tom seeks his family and tries to make sense of a world gone mad. At the same time he finds himself relentlessly hunted by the same dark forces he encountered before his accident. His only hope seems to lie with the members of an underground resistance lead by Helen Hanna (Leigh Lewis) who are trying to expose this Messiah as the devil himself. Tom is suddenly caught in the middle of a battle old as time in which the very souls of mankind hang in the balance.

"Delivers a powerful, thought-provoking message wrapped in an exciting package of action and suspense."

Available at your favorite bookstore.

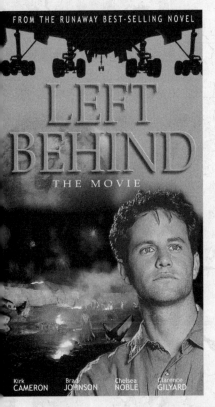